Solstice Goat

A Patricia Fisher Blue Moon Mystery

Book 1

Steve Higgs

Dedication

This book is dedicated to Erin Hayes. Thank you for reading, Erin.

Table of Contents

Part of the Community

The Body of Gerard Gallagher

The Bookshop

Dogs and Cars

Mortice Keys

Observe

Pagan Ritual

Friends

Clues and the Mayor

Clues

Breakfast

Old Books

The Goat-Headed God

CHP

Low Point

Research

Breaking and Entering

The Big Clue

Kicking the Wasp's Nest

Final Piece of the Puzzle

Party Crashers

The Lord Mayor

Race Against Time

The Bomb

Terrible News

Ray of Hope

The Church Council

Busted

The Mob

Human Sacrifice

A Humble Apology

More Books by Steve Higgs

Even More Books by Steve Higgs

Author Note:

Free Books and More

Part of the Community

Right after service on a Sunday morning, I was sitting in the village hall at a meeting of the church council. I joined just a couple of days ago when I learned that Angelica Howard-Box had taken over as the president. She and I have some history and I know that she is a devious cow with a power-mad streak who will bully the other members of the church council, mostly older men and women, into doing things the way she thought they ought to be done. Our vicar, Geoffrey Grey, wasn't a young man either and unlikely to fight her I thought.

This was my first meeting and Angelica was standing in front of the rest of the seated church council members dictating what flowers were and were not appropriate for display in the church. Apparently, freesias were unconditionally banned.

'But I have always displayed freesias,' argued Betty Wilshaw, an octogenarian who lived to grow and display flowers in the church.

Angelica fixed her with a glare. 'Betty, we agreed that if a person wanted to speak, they would raise their hand and not just interrupt whoever has the chair. Otherwise these meetings will return to the chaos they have always been.'

I didn't bother to put my hand up. 'We didn't agree at all, Angelica. You announced that it was what you wanted and moved on. The council gets to vote.'

'But you do not, Patricia,' she snapped, trying to quell the uprising before it got started. 'You are a probationary member and do not get to vote or even have an opinion yet.'

1

'That's not a thing,' I countered. Then, to Roy, a retired RAF Wing Commander sitting next to me, I whispered from the corner of my mouth, 'Is it?'

'It never was before,' he whispered back and then more loudly, because he wasn't shy at being forward, he said, 'We don't have probationary members, Angelica.'

'It's a new thing I am introducing,' she replied with a smile as if that was supposed to win us all over. 'It's point one hundred and twelve on my list – probationary members do not get to have a say in how the church is run for the first two years of their membership. Now if you would all focus, take notes as previously asked, and stop interrupting, I could get past point six which we appear to have got stuck on.'

My phone rang just as I started to argue. It was supposed to be switched to silent of course but I had forgotten yet again. It continued to ring unabated as I frantically rummaged to find the infernal thing and switch it off.

As I grasped it and finally thumbed the button, I could feel Angelica's glare. When I looked up, she raged. 'Probationary members are not allowed to bring phones to meetings of the church council!' She and I were old enemies which stemmed from an incident at school when we were eight years old: I stole her boyfriend. She has never forgiven me, and over the decades I had actively encouraged her hatred. My problem now was that she was not only the president of the church council but also the local parish councillor and I felt certain she was going to use both positions to make my life miserable if she possibly could.

I chose not to return her glare; I was in the wrong this time after all, but couldn't help but notice the name displayed on my phone was that of Mike Atwell, a detective sergeant with the local constabulary which covered the area which included my village. He and I were becoming good friends, but he only called when he had something of significance to tell me, so I pressed the button to answer the call, whispered into it, and with an oops expression at the wing commander, I slipped out of the village hall.

My name is Patricia Fisher. I'm a middle-aged woman with a mediocre education, no qualifications, and I am soon to be divorced. My blonde hair is slowly filling with grey, I have wrinkles appearing at the corners of my eyes and around my mouth, and they will not go away no matter how much ceramide boosting night cream I apply. A few months ago, I was a self-employed cleaner, going to other people's houses to deal with their mess while I ignored the mess my life had become. Then, a stroke of fate sent me on an around the world cruise which changed my life irrevocably. Now, I am a private investigator. I live in a seventy-three-room mansion, and I have my own butler.

As I reached the door to the church and slipped outside, I pressed the button to return Mike's call. It connected instantly.

'Hello, Patricia. Did I disturb you?'

'I was in church. I assume you have something newsworthy to tell me.' I have several ongoing cases I am being paid to investigate, some of which will undoubtedly warrant the attention of the police when I solve them. While in theory I can perform a citizen's arrest on a criminal just the same as anyone else, in practice, I am a relatively petite fifty-three-year-old woman with no special fighting skills, so when it came time to cart someone off to jail, I did the sensible thing and called the professionals. Mike liked our relationship because I kept making him look good.

'You are looking for a missing couple, aren't you? Helena and Gerard Gallagher?'

'Yes,' I replied tentatively, unsure I wanted to hear what he was going to say next.

'I'm afraid his body was just identified. I'm on my way to the scene now.'

I huffed out a breath of frustration. My client is a man named Jerry Brock. He is the father of Helena Gallagher and the one who reported the couple as missing a week ago. At the time, there was nothing to suggest they had done anything other than decide to go away. As the days went on with no response from them, even the police had to accept their disappearance was suspicious, but there appeared to be no trail to follow. He hired me just a couple of days ago, but so far, I wasn't having much luck in tracking down what might have happened to them. Now I had a dead body.

'Where is it?' I asked.

'In the woods near Upnor. If you park near the yacht club, you can walk along. I'm told it's about one hundred yards once you get onto the beach and just into the woods from there.'

A quick mental calculation told me it would take half an hour at least to get there and I really wasn't dressed for walking along a muddy beach and into overgrown woodland. Add on a little time to get changed and I needed to get moving right now. I really wanted to get back inside the village hall to do battle with Angelica, but this had to take priority. I told him, 'I'm on my way,' as I took my car keys from my bag.

With the phone away, my hurried steps took me to my car, a 1954 Aston Martin DB2/4 Drophead Coupé in silver with a tan leather interior. I had a choice of cars, but this was the one I preferred to drive; it was just so elegant and refined. If you are wondering if I am filthily rich and thus questioning why I need to visit dead bodies on a Sunday when I could be

4

doing much nicer things, then the answer is both simple and complex. My cruise around the world brought me into contact with the Maharaja of Zangrabar, the third richest man in the world. I sort of saved his life and he, in turn, gave me a house. He said he no longer wanted it because it was too far from London for his purposes. It wasn't just a house, though, it was a massive estate with a mansion at its centre. It came with staff and a garage full of cars and every bill is paid for in perpetuity. So, I don't really have any money, but I look and feel like I am super rich.

I fired the engine to life with a roar and set off for home.

I arrived in Upnor dressed in jeans, walking boots and a wax jacket. It had taken me over an hour to get there, but I wasn't concerned that I might be too late; these things always take ages, as the police crime scene team catalogued and photographed and meticulously inspected every blade of grass.

I hadn't visited the tiny hamlet of Upnor on the banks of the river Medway in years. So long, in fact, that I couldn't remember when I last had. Nothing much had changed though. Upnor sits on the north bank of the river Medway overlooking Chatham and St Mary's Island on the other side. It boasts two pubs and a yacht club and a small Royal Engineers outpost. I found a space next to a red Porsche in the free-to-use public carpark, my dog, Anna, popping her head up to see where we were when she sensed that I had stopped.

'Come on, girl,' I said as I scooped her. Anna is a shaded red miniature dachshund who I came by during my brief excursion to Tokyo, yet another stop on my cruise and yet another destination where I found myself in all kinds of trouble.

She started pulling on her lead the second her feet hit the ground, trying to go somewhere and not worrying too much where it might be as long as she could get there quickly. A few gentle tugs got her going in the right direction, but the detailed description Mike gave me for how to find the site wasn't needed because there were cops everywhere. I had seen their cars on the way in but now I was heading along the path to the beach, I could see their bright reflective jackets ahead of me.

Police barrier tape formed a perimeter to keep people back but the only people likely to come here were those who wanted to walk their dogs. It was a grey day, and cooler than it had been, my Barbour wax jacket doing its job to keep me warm. The leaves were all turning and beginning to drop, a small blanket of them covering the mud and rocks of the shore until the next high tide later today when they would be washed away.

Seeing me approach, a young female police officer came to the barrier tape to stop me. 'Sorry, ma'am, you'll have to turn around.'

I was going to ask her to find DS Atwell, but he appeared from the trees behind her, the text message I sent five minutes ago to announce my arrival doing the trick nicely.

'She's with me,' he called as he jogged across the beach.

Seeing no need for comment, the officer in uniform held the tape up for me to pass under, Anna pulling me along again as she tried to get to Mike.

I gave him a smile as he stopped to pet the tiny dog before she could climb his legs with her muddy paws. 'Good morning, Mike. Thanks for the call,' I said.

He gave me a grim expression in return. 'You might want to hold onto your thanks until you have seen it. It's not nice.'

I consider it a statement about how much my life has changed that I no longer think anything of seeing a dead body. When I saw my first one, a man called Jack Langley, on board the cruise ship, I was fascinated more than I was repulsed. He had been murdered with a knife to his back, and I had seen many bodies since with far worse injuries. Mike wasn't wrong though. This was something else. As we approached, I picked Anna up so she wouldn't affect the crime scene.

Gerard Gallagher had been arranged in death so that he would be found posed the way his killer wanted him. He was sitting in a chair which had been fashioned from twigs and branches, woven together much like a bird makes its nest. It was crude, but strong enough to support his dead weight. He was naked and his body was covered in odd symbols I didn't recognise, or at least couldn't name, but wanted to say were wiccan in origin. They were daubed on with a dark paint, the size of each mark making me think they were put on with someone's finger. Those on his lower abdomen were mostly obscured by blood from a wound to his chest, but I couldn't really see it because two men were blocking my view.

The first of them had seen me coming and was facing me now. 'Mrs Fisher,' said the man in greeting. I hadn't paid him any attention thus far, too busy looking around him at the awful sight to see his face. Now that he had my attention, I saw that I knew him.

'Hello, Simon.' He was one of a pair of crime scene guys I had met just a few days ago. His partner, Steven turned his head around from examining the body to give me a wave.

'Who found him?' I asked Mike, keeping my voice low and staying back as there were a dozen officers all performing tasks and I didn't want to get in the way.

'A lady by the name of Greta Holford. Her golden retriever, Max, found him at seven this morning. She was walking him along the beach, but he ran into the woods and then wouldn't stop barking and wouldn't come back. She came into the woods to see what he had found.'

'Was he killed here?' I asked.

Steven heard me and stood up. He had been kneeling by the victim, taking samples of soil but stopped to answer my question. He was roughly my age and almost completely bald. What hair remained was cut close to

8

his scalp. He and Simon looked like they could be brothers, but I knew it was Steven addressing me because he wore glasses.

'The victim was killed by massive trauma to his heart,' he explained. 'He was stabbed with a knife that has a circular, Kris-style blade ...' he saw the question form on my face. 'Kris-style means the blade is wavy rather than straight. It was a single blow that punctured his heart. We will know more once the autopsy has been conducted but the murder was committed here between eleven last night and one this morning. He was then arranged post-mortem. The chair was constructed from material gathered here and each piece was broken not cut though I cannot tell you if that has any significance.'

The more he told me, the more questions I had. 'Can you identify the symbols?'

'They're pagan.' The answer came from behind me, Mike and I both turning around to see who had spoken.

Standing just above us at the crest of a small rise was a man. He observed the scene in a manner that made me think very little escaped his attention. His blue eyes kept moving, roving around to take in everything there was to see. In contrast to the police, who were either in uniform or wearing functional, but cheap suits as befitted the role, this man wore casual office clothes; tan jeans and leather brogues beneath a light blue cotton oxford shirt and a navy-blue windbreaker. His facial hair was longer than the last time I saw him, but I recognised him straight away. He was the owner of a rival investigation firm and a former soldier. He was tall and good-looking, with a neat and recent haircut and a well-trimmed beard. His age somewhere in his late thirties, I judged.

'Hello, Tempest.'

He shot me a tight smile, anything more would have been inappropriate in this setting, and closed the distance to shake my hand. 'Hello again, Patricia.' Tempest switched his focus to Mike as he was standing next to me. 'Hello, I'm Tempest Michaels.'

'DS Mike Atwell. I have heard of you, of course.' The two men exchanged a handshake before Tempest brought his gaze back to me.

'Are you investigating?' he asked.

'I am. My client is this man's father-in-law,' I supplied as I indicated the victim.

Tempest nodded, stepping around me to get a closer look.

Simon was waiting for him. 'Morning, Tempest. I suppose I shouldn't be surprised that you are here, this one has weird written all over it. You say you recognise the symbols?'

Tempest nodded. 'The symbology at least. It's not wiccan.'

'What's the difference?' Mike asked, moving closer and genuinely interested to hear the answer.

Tempest was biting his lip and staring at the symbols but stepped back so he could explain. 'Wicca is a tradition of witchcraft that was brought to the public by Gerald Gardner in the 1950s. There is a great deal of debate among the Pagan community about whether or not wicca is truly the same form of witchcraft that the ancients practiced. Regardless, many people use the terms wicca and witchcraft interchangeably. Paganism is an umbrella term used to apply to a number of different earth-based faiths. Wicca falls under that heading, although not all pagans are wiccan. So, all wiccans are witches, but not all witches are wiccans. All wiccans are pagans, but not all pagans are wiccans. Finally, *some* witches are pagans, but some are not - and some pagans practice witchcraft, while others choose not to.'

'Good. Glad I asked. Not confusing at all,' Mike replied flippantly.

'You can think of it as different languages. French, German and English all use the same alphabet, but the words are different. Wiccan symbols are very similar to pagan symbols but used differently with different meanings.' He pointed to Gerard's shoulder. 'This symbol is balefire. Traditionally it means a large open fire and has been scrambled in modern usage, so we now say bonfire, but when used in conjunction with the widdershins symbol next to it - you can see there is a line joining them - it means a powerful weapon of some sort. I think. I need to check with someone.' He had a faraway look to his eyes already as if he were lost in thought and no longer really here with us. As he moved away, heading back to the shore, he threw us all a wave. 'Nice meeting you, Mike. Good luck with your investigation, Patricia.'

I raced after him, putting Anna down once I was clear of the cordoned off area. 'Tempest, wait,' I called to stop him. He was ten yards ahead of me and on his way back to the carpark area. He stopped to wait for me though. 'Are you investigating this as well?' I asked him.

'Yes. It's an old case of mine actually. I was looking into two young women who went missing last year. It was about ten months ago now, quite close to the winter solstice. I was on the trail of what I believed was a group of pagan magic practitioners but suddenly they were gone; all their activity ceased, and I failed to close the case or find the women. Then they showed up dead a few weeks later. I don't know if this is the same group, it has all the hallmarks, but they were not inscribed like the latest victim. Either way, I am going to find out who is behind this and put a stop to it.'

He sounded like an action hero from a movie; utterly determined and resolute. I also believed he was going to do what he said, and it gave me an idea. 'Can we join forces?'

He raised an eyebrow. 'You mean combine our resources and work on this together?' He pushed his lips out as he ran the idea through his head. 'I don't see why we shouldn't. Two heads and all that. I'm on my way to see a chap in Rochester. He's something of an expert in all things weird. Do you want to tag along?'

The idea of working with another P.I. enthralled me, truth be told. I always felt that I bumbled through my cases, looking for clues that would help me to work out what had happened, so working with someone who had been doing it for longer and probably in a very different way might be an education.

I said, 'Sure. My car's in the car park.'

'Mine too,' he replied and the pair of us started walking again, Anna leading the way as always, and we chatted about my little dog and her puppies until we got to the carpark.

'This is yours?' he asked, pointing to my Aston Martin with a whistle of appreciation. 'Nice wheels.' Before I could reply, he slid into the red Porsche parked next to mine. I popped Anna on the passenger's seat in a special chair made to keep a small doggy safe in a car. It also kept her muddy feet from my supple leather upholstery. We were both heading to Rochester High Street where Tempest was taking me to see a man called Frank Decaux.

The Bookshop

It transpired that Frank Decaux worked in a bookshop. Or, more precisely, he owned a bookshop. It was just around the corner from my office, no more than one hundred yards and just along from the ancient North Gate where citizens visiting the city would gain access many centuries ago.

It was a funny little place I had driven by a few times without noticing it was there. The entrance was a nondescript door which led to a set of wooden stairs where I passed framed pictures of the Loch Ness Monster, Big Foot, a UFO, and many more besides. The sign on the door told me the place was called The Mystery Men, and the whole experience was confusing me because I thought I was going to meet an expert in the occult, not visit a bookstore.

In spite of my reservations, the shop was popular, full to the brim almost with men and women across a range of ages. There were long and high wooden bookshelves running perpendicular to the counter, the one facing me contained rows of non-fiction books covering a wealth of topics but all to do with the supernatural or occult. I spotted a display stand with comic books to my left and a glass cabinet that contained figures from popular movies next to it. Once inside, I placed Anna on the floor so she could move around but kept her lead short so she would be close to me and not be accidentally stepped on.

Tempest led me into the small store and over to the counter where a young Chinese woman was serving two teenage boys. Her fringe was cut on a diagonal slant, her natural black hair showing a bright pink colour beneath which peeked out all around the edge as if she had two layers of hair.

Ahead of me, Tempest said, 'Hi, Poison. Is Frank in?'

13

I noted that her name badge did indeed claim her name to be Poison. She didn't answer him, she just turned her head and shouted through the door behind her, 'Frank!'

A man's voice echoed back. 'Do you need me?'

'Your favourite paranormal investigator is here!' she yelled, then stabbed the till with a red talon and took the twenty pound note the boy was offering her. Once she thanked them and told them she hoped they came back soon, her voice a husky, flirtatious whisper, she finally looked up at Tempest. 'Still got a girlfriend?' she asked.

He laughed. 'Yes, thank you, Poison. I will let you know if that goes wrong.'

'You be sure to,' she murmured before leaving the counter to help a customer who wanted to more closely inspect a figure in the glass cabinet.

Footsteps echoing through from the gap behind the counter preceded a man appearing. He was scruffy but in a tidy way, if that makes any sense. What I mean is, he appeared to have done his best but didn't have much to work with. He was short at about five feet five inches and his clothes seemed to hang off him as if they just didn't make clothes that fit his shape. He peered at the pair of us from behind thick glasses which looked almost too big for his head. I judged that he was in his early forties, he was unmarried, if the lack of wedding band was reliable, and he was smiling like an idiot.

'Whatcha, Tempest. How's the paranormal debunking business going?' Then he noticed me. 'Goodness, you're Patricia Fisher.'

'Yes, I am.' I extended my hand and we shook. 'You are Frank Decaux, I believe.'

14

'Indeed I am. Welcome to my humble bookshop. Now,' he said, clapping his hands together and rubbing them gleefully. 'Tempest only comes in here when he wants to know something, so let's cut to the chase shall we?'

That's exactly what Tempest did. 'Frank, a man was murdered last night. Stabbed in the heart with a Kris-style knife in what looks like a ritual sacrifice. His body had pagan symbols daubed on it. What're your thoughts?'

Frank cupped his chin for a moment. Then he pushed between us to get to the shelf with the non-fiction books on it. 'It really depends whether your assessment of the symbols is accurate, which symbols they were and how they were presented.' From the bottom shelf he grasped a huge book that looked to weigh twenty pounds. 'Wode's Paganology will give us the answers.'

The book hit the counter with a loud bang and he instantly flipped it open to roughly halfway and then started turning pages until he got to the one he wanted.

Tempest stopped him just as he stopped anyway, jabbing his finger into the page. 'Widdershins, Frank. The victim had widdershins on his left deltoid.'

'So, it's probably pagan. What other symbols did he have?'

Tempest's voice took on a dread tone when he next spoke, locking eyes with Frank so he knew he had something serious to say. 'Frank, it was linked to balefire.' A heartbeat passed as neither man spoke. Then Frank swallowed. 'It's them again, isn't it?' Tempest asked.

Frank looked down at the page of symbols again and back up before saying, 'Yes. I think it might be.'

I had to interrupt. 'Sorry, gentlemen. Can one of you tell me what the significance of the symbols is and who it is that you think we might be chasing?'

'My apologies,' said Tempest, taking a step back so that I was more included in what the two men were looking at. 'Frank, do you want to talk about the symbols?' he suggested.

Frank drummed his fingers on the page of the book and then swung it around so it faced me. 'The two symbols are inherently pagan in origin though many of the pagan practitioners these days are not terribly well educated in the practices they use and mix symbols up any old how. Either one of them has no particular meaning by itself. Widdershins for example just means against the rotation of the sun. It can be used to mean going backwards in time though or simply to reverse an action. When linked with balefire, it suggests whatever magic is being conjured is to be used as a weapon. I have only ever heard of the two symbols being used like this once before and that was when Tempest reported it to me a year ago.'

Tempest took out his phone and scrolled through his pictures. When he found the one he wanted, he handed the phone to me and leaned in to show me what it was. 'I took this from the site where they found the first of the women's bodies. I didn't think anything of it until they found the second woman and the same symbols were present there too.' The same symbols I had seen on Gerard's shoulder were spray painted onto a brick wall, rivulets of paint running down from each symbol and from the small line joining them.

'I'm not an expert on paganism,' Frank admitted. 'You want to speak to Mortice Keys in Canterbury. He'll be able to tell you a lot more about what this might mean. '

'Wait a moment,' I raised my hand. 'Mortice Keys is a person's name?'

'Yes,' replied Frank. 'Actually, his real name is Arthur Poole, but he hasn't responded to that name for years. He used to be the head of the Kent League of Demonologists until they revolted and threw him out for being too radical.'

I mouthed the sentence Frank had just used; certain I had heard him correctly but startled by all the new concepts I was hearing today. Pagan sacrifices, people with weird fake names, and now a league of demonologists. It felt like I was the butt of a practical joke.

However, the strangeness of our conversation wasn't bothering Tempest at all. He asked, 'Do you have an address for him?'

'Sure. You can even find him in the Yellow Pages. He has a shop in Canterbury. He's a prickly one though, he won't tell you a thing if he doesn't think you are a believer. You'll have to convince him. Or, you know, take Big Ben and have him threaten the man until he talks.'

'I'm sure he'll talk to me, Frank,' Tempest replied with a smile. 'I'm a trustworthy guy.'

Dogs and Cars

I got a call from Barbie as I was leaving the bookshop. A light drizzle had set in, making us hurry along the High Street to get back to our cars when her voice came on the line.

'Hey, Patty. Where are you? I thought we were having lunch today?' Barbie is a young woman from Los Angeles who I met on the cruise ship. She was one of the gym instructors and has the kind of tight, toned, flawless body most women would kill for. She also has flowing, perfectly straight, natural blond hair and the kind of chest that causes drivers to crash their cars. When I got off the ship after my cruise, she followed me to my new house and now lives with me. Her boyfriend, a junior doctor she met in Tokyo, works at St Barts in London, but when she asked if she could crash at my place until she found her own, I insisted she stay. It wasn't like I didn't have the room to spare.

I told her, 'I got a lead on one of my cases, so I set off to investigate.'

'Oh, that's good,' she said encouragingly.

I had to pull a face. 'It's not, actually. It's that missing couple case. The husband turned up dead last night.'

Barbie gasped. 'Oh, God. No sign of the missing woman?'

'None yet, but they have been missing for more than a week and he was murdered last night so maybe they still have her.'

'Do you have any idea who *they* are?'

With a sigh of my own, I admitted, 'Not yet. I'm working with another detective though. A chap called Tempest Michaels. You might have heard me talk about him.'

She thought about that for a second. 'No. No, it's not ringing any bells. Look Jermaine and I are heading into Kings Hill for some lunch. I expect we will be there a while if you get the chance to join us.' I told her I was on my way to Canterbury and wouldn't be back for a while. 'Are you taking Anna with you?'

Oh, bother. I hadn't thought about that. It was nice to have her with me, but she tended to get grumpy if I kept her out too long; she liked to sleep. I said goodbye to Barbie and looked down at my dog.

'Problem?' asked Tempest, seeing that I had stopped and coming back to check on me. He followed my eyes down to Anna, who gave a quick wag of her tail as she looked up at us.

'I need to drop this one at home,' I said, my tone expressing that I wasn't keen to delay moving our investigation forward.

'Where's home?' he asked.

'West Malling,' I told him with a grimace. It wasn't that far to go but it was in totally the opposite direction.

Then he thought of an idea. 'Do you want to leave her with my dogs? It will be like a play date. He pointed to a wall. 'They're in my office right now with one of the other detectives and the office assistant.'

I thought about it for a moment but couldn't come up with a reason not to. He led me to a door in the back of his office and down a long corridor which led to another door. On the other side of that was an office about twenty times the size of mine. It was a large space with two private offices at one end, a reception area near the door with a lady sitting at a desk, and a waiting area with a couple of couches and a coffee machine.

The moment we were through the door, two sausage shapes appeared from one of the private offices. As a blur, they shot across the floor in the direction of their owner and then saw Anna which caused them to change direction swiftly. The three dogs were instantly all over each other as everyone tried to sniff someone else. I had to fight to keep Anna still long enough to get her collar off.

'Hi, Tempest,' said a lean blonde woman as she came out of the office behind the dogs.

'Hi, Jane. This is Patricia Fisher.' A sweep of his arm made it clear he was talking about me and not the dog.

We shook hands. 'Hello, I'm Jane Butterworth,' she said. 'Well, most of the time.' I raised an eyebrow wondering what that comment meant. It seemed like an odd thing to say, but she didn't follow it up with any more information and Tempest asked her a question.

'Any luck with the wizard case?'

She shrugged. 'Maybe. I keep hitting dead ends. It's like he vanishes in a puff of smoke.' She laughed at her own joke.

Tempest groaned. 'Will you be going out? I have to go to Canterbury and want to leave the dogs here a little longer. Is that going to work out?'

Jane said, 'I think I'll be doing research for the rest of the day, but Marjory will be here if I need to pop out.'

'I'm Marjory,' called the lady on the reception desk with a wave of her hand even though she didn't take her eyes from her screen.

'Super,' said Tempest. 'We shouldn't be long. Can you do me a favour, though? Can you find a man called Mortice Keys and send me a photograph and whatever else you can find out about him, please?'

Jane grinned and wiggled her eyebrows. 'That's what I do best.'

I looked down as a blur went by my feet. The three dogs were playing chase and wrestling, having a great time already. I had never left her with anyone else, but I had a feeling she was going to enjoy her afternoon, so I waved goodbye to the ladies and went back outside.

'Your car or mine?' I asked.

'Yours, if that's okay,' he said, eyeing my Aston eagerly. 'I thought about getting myself a vintage Aston Martin a few times, but I love my little Porsche. Maybe I'll be forced to part with it at some point, but I am dying to have a look at yours.'

It was an honest answer, so we took mine, Tempest admiring the craftwork on the interior as I started her up. His phone pinged and he laughed. When he saw my questioning look, he said, 'That's an email from Jane.' He pulled the phone from his pocket to prove it. 'It's been what? Eighty seconds since I asked her for information and here it is already.'

I had to admit that I was impressed. 'She's very pretty,' I observed, going fishing since Poison at the bookshop had talked about his girlfriend and I wondered if the two of them might be involved.

'I suppose,' he replied. 'She's not really my type.' I raised an eyebrow when I didn't really mean to, but he saw it and explained his comment. 'Jane is … Jane is a boy. She's gender neutral or gender fluid or … you know I'm not sure what the correct term is, but that is what she has going on. So, yes, she's pretty but some days she comes to work as a man called James and has all the right bits to make him a man.'

21

I wanted to let my jaw drop. Not because I was shocked by the concept. I wasn't. What surprised me was how convincing she had looked and sounded. I would never have worked it out for myself, but I was glad I knew now because it would have thrown me for a loop if I met the man version one day without knowing.

As we cruised down the M2 motorway to Canterbury, Tempest told me what Jane had been able to turn up on Mortice Keys and we discussed how we were going to get the man to spill the goods on the symbols.

Much like Rochester, where our offices are located, Canterbury is an ancient city filled with architecture that is hundreds of years old. In between buildings and along the side of the road leading into the centre of the city, the old city wall can be seen, preserved now by government funding no doubt but surviving the ravages of time because it was built to keep out invading hordes and is thus rather sturdy.

Mr Mortice Keys owned a small shop just off the central business district in the centre of the city. It sat in the shadow of the cathedral where it undoubtedly attracted plenty of passing trade. Earth Magic was my second odd little shop of the day, I observed, as the bell jingled above my head to announce that customers had entered the shop.

We knew from the picture Jane supplied that Mr Keys was a large man. He came into the shop from a back room, his stomach leading the way as it strained against his belt. Not that I could see his belt. His chin hung low beneath his jaw where it tiered into his chest. He had a full head of hair which was the colour and texture of wheat. It sat, like an unkempt mop, above his face which was a confusion of thin red veins and glowing red cheeks as if he were permanently embarrassed. Two small blue eyes poked out to take us in as he flourished his hands theatrically.

'Greetings, travellers. Are you practitioners in need of my fine ingredients? Or followers looking for artefacts that may assist you to attune your spirits with the eldritch gods so that you may commune with the ancients?'

I opened my mouth to reply, but Tempest beat me to it. 'We are followers, great one. We sought out your fabled apothecary for advice and supplies. We wish to commune with our forebears and learn of their secrets. Through them we will achieve long and healthy lives. We must purchase all that you have to sell.'

'Yes! Yes!' Mortice replied, his eyes alight with excitement. I mimicked Tempest, feeling a little silly, but holding my arms out to my sides as he was and bending into a bow from the waist.

'We beg of you knowledge,' I cried, my voice almost an imploring wail. 'We travelled far to learn from you.'

'Come to me, disciples of the true Earth faith. Let us discuss your needs and method of payment.'

As he turned away, Tempest winked at me. Then whispered, 'I've met a load of the Earth magic people in the past. They are all the same; if you talk their language, they welcome you in with open arms. Plus, this guy thinks we are going to buy his junk so he's especially friendly.'

Mortice Keys had finally dropped his arms and was now beginning to show us around the shop. However, as he tried to sell his goods to us, Tempest made his sales pitch pointless by taking items off the shelves and out of the window display to place them on the counter. The shopkeeper's eyes were bugging from his head with glee as his brain mentally calculated the profit.

'You have so many wonderful artefacts,' Tempest praised the man as he placed a ram's skull on the top of the pile. Tempest had no intention of buying any of these items, of course, we had bet on being able to lull the fool into a state where he would tell us anything.

'And you have a good eye, sir,' gushed Mortice. 'That skull is from a Tibetan Crossback Ram. It was blessed by the Mage at the Temple of Eternal Karma himself. It will bring luck to your household.'

He certainly knew how to spin a yarn, but it was my turn now. Tempest had him thoroughly distracted so I drew Mr Keys' attention back to me. 'We wish to mark our house with symbology that will lead spirits to us and ensure our dwelling is blessed by the seasons and by the night and kept free of evil intentions that might invade as we sleep. Can you help me? I believe I have selected all the correct power runes to mark the four corners but friends of ours were struck by a terrible sickness when they got their marking wrong. Can you check my symbology, please?'

'Of course, child,' he cooed. 'You have, of course, drawn the Earth mother above your hearth?'

'Yes, and the horned man is marked beneath the carpets to keep him in the soil.'

'Very good.' Mortice replied as Tempest brought yet more items to the counter; the pile now almost too high to see over.

'What of this symbol?' Tempest asked, showing widdershins and balefire which he'd drawn previously onto a blank page in his notebook. 'Will this bring success and power to our house?'

Mortice Keys dropped his act instantly. Like a switch being thrown, his voice changed from well-spoken, kindly uncle to rough east-end criminal. His face became a sneer as he growled. 'Who the bleep are you two?

Calmly, Tempest said, 'There is a lady present. Please mind your language.'

Mortice's eyes bugged out. 'You better get the bleep out of my bleeping shop right this bleeping minute or you'll find out what it feels like to bleeping …' His rant was cut off by Tempest slapping his face. It wasn't a hard slap, but it wasn't a playful one either.

'I'm sorry, Patricia,' Tempest said, taking my hand and turning toward the door. 'I don't make a habit of teaching manners, but his choice of verbs was a bit much.'

Mortice wasn't done though, he roared his outrage and rushed after us, dodging around the counter to get to Tempest faster than I would have given him credit for.

Tempest let go of my hand to face his adversary, saying, 'I advise against this course of action, sir.'

Mortice Keys wasn't listening though, he had his head down and he was charging, the whole shop shaking each time one of his feet hit the floor. The string of expletives ended abruptly when he got to Tempest, and the smaller man converted Mortice's forward momentum into a throw.

Mortice tumbled, arms and legs flailing as he went over Tempest's hip and spun in the air to land on his back. I think Tempest was as gentle as he could be, and he then checked the larger man was alright before he straightened and took a pace back. Of course, I had seen my butler, Jermaine, fight several times in the past. Jermaine was part ninja or something, and Barbie's boyfriend, Hideki, was a certified martial arts master, but Tempest knew how to move and was calm throughout the encounter which told me he had training too.

'Sorry about that,' he apologised to me as he straightened up. 'Shall we go?'

Outside the shop we hurried to a corner and then turned to watch. 'Did you see his face when you showed him the symbols?' I asked. Tempest nodded. 'It was abject fear.' The back of my skull was itching because I had just seen something that was connected to the case. I didn't know how yet, but Mr Mortice Keys was involved. 'I think we should watch him and see what he does next.'

Tempest said, 'I concur,' with a nod. 'Something about the symbols spooked him. He recognised them and knew what they mean to the people behind whatever is going on.'

'Do you think he might be directly involved?'

Tempest shrugged. 'No sense in conjecture until we know more.'

I nodded my head across the street where a small café had an empty table in the window. 'I could do with some lunch. Shall we watch from over there?'

'I'll meet you in there. I'm going to check around the back and see if there is another way out. I also want to see what car he drives so we will know if he leaves in it.'

By the time he returned, I had a pot of tea and a cheese sandwich in front of me, and the same for Tempest, expecting that he would be hungry too. Both sandwiches were packed to go in paper bags just in case we needed to leave before we got the chance to eat them. I needn't have bothered; it was more than an hour before Mortice Keys appeared again. We saw him in the window at the front of his shop. He glanced left and right and then turned the open sign around so it read closed. He locked the door, rattled it to make sure it wasn't going to open and vanished back into the gloom. Then the light inside switched off. It was a little after three in the afternoon, no time to be closing up so he was up to something and our hunch had paid off.

We were going to tail him to wherever he was going and hope that it led us closer to solving the case. Not for the first time, I had no idea I was about to place myself in grave danger.

Observe

Mortice Keys drove a Jaguar S Type. It was black and easy to spot which was good because I had to tail it through Canterbury traffic which had quadrupled since we arrived. I had to jump the lights when he slipped through two cars ahead of me and they changed before I could get there. Luck was on my side and no cop car was around to see my misdemeanour.

He was as blithely unaware as Tempest expected he would be, never once checking his rear-view mirror. It wasn't my first time tailing someone, but it was my first time doing it while also driving the car and I found my adrenalin was through the roof.

It's not far from Canterbury town centre to the motorway which he joined, indicating in plenty of time and cruising down the on-ramp to feed into light traffic. I hung back a little further since it was easy to see his big car and he kept to the speed limit and indicated each time he changed lane to go around a truck.

Ten minutes, twenty minutes, then thirty ticked by as we came back into familiar territory closer to where we lived. Then, just as I started to wonder if he was going to drive all the way into the centre of London which is where the motorway ended, his indicator came on and he moved onto a slip road. Now on the A249, he would pass dozens of small villages and the larger town of Sittingbourne before reaching the Island of Sheppey just off the coast. He could be going to any one of them, but five minutes later he turned off onto the A2 which narrowed the list of possible destinations. This was a rural area and the roads were single track with fields on either side. I wanted to keep my distance but yet again my car was directly behind his. As I began to drop back, Tempest said, 'You'll have to stay close now. If he turns off, we could lose him. Better to be spotted than to have wasted our afternoon.'

I had to agree but my concern that he might notice the very distinct silver car on his tail was unwarranted because he never once flicked his eyes at his mirrors. The fields changed to woodland on either side, high trees forming a canopy above our heads until we reached the hamlet of Newington. Just after that, he turned off the A road down a wide track through the woods and we carried onwards, the satellite map on Tempest's phone showing him that the country lane Mortice had taken went for a mile but then terminated. What was at the end of the road the satellite image didn't show us. It just showed a grey box which was representative of a building.

'We'll need to walk, won't we?' I asked though I already knew the answer. To see what he was up to we needed to be stealthy the rest of the way.

Tempest nodded. 'I can take it from here.' He held up his hands defensively. 'I'm not suggesting anything that could be considered chauvinistic; I'm trained for this kind of thing, that's all. If you want to come, that's fine too.'

He dealt with the issue cleverly, giving me the option to head home with only the barest suggestion that I might slow him down, but made no attempt to convince me. 'I think I'll tag along, if that's okay?'

In reply, he looked down at his leather loafers and said, 'I should have worn better shoes.'

We parked my car in Newington at the end of a residential street. It would stick out because it was the type of car that stuck out everywhere. However, I doubted anyone would mess with it in such a rural setting so we set off to walk, but not along the path. Tempest, the former solider that he is, was going to be invisible in his approach so was going cross country. I had already committed to doing it his way, so I offered no argument and was thankful I chose jeans when I left the house earlier.

It was a mercy that the weather chose to be kind to us and we hadn't seen rain in more than a week, other than the odd drizzle which didn't look to have reached this part of the country because the soil beneath our feet was dry and parched. Nevertheless, it was a slog to get to our target, Tempest navigating through the trees as if he knew exactly where he was going even though he had no map or compass. When I asked him how he was doing it, because I was hopelessly lost, he claimed to be using the topography – navigating by contours having memorised the map from his phone.

It was uphill almost the entire way, the building itself not becoming visible until we crested the rise just two hundred yards short of the target. The trees thinned out and gave way to open fields. They were not cultivated, but just growing wild with meadow flowers peeking above rough grasses and gorse bushes dotted here and there. The lack of trees meant we could see all the way down to the building. What we saw was unexpected.

It was an abandoned industrial plant.

There had been no signs in the road and the trees and shrubbery growing up between the buildings told us it had been empty for many years. The black Jaguar wasn't the only car visible inside the fence line. Mortice was here to meet others.

'What now?' I asked Tempest, this part of it was his show after all.

'Now we wait,' he replied. 'They won't be able to see us from here and it will be dark in a couple of hours. Whatever Mr Keys is up to, I doubt very much we are witnessing a choral society meeting down there. We should eat and rest a while and let people know where we are.'

'Yes. I need to arrange for Jermaine to collect Anna. I'm sure she has had a wonderful playdate, but it will be her dinner time soon.'

'Is that your partner?' Tempest asked.

I smiled, knowing where the conversation was about to go. 'No. Jermaine is my butler.' To my surprise, Tempest just nodded, accepting that I had a butler without comment. 'Really?' I prompted. 'You don't want to know more?'

My question got a sly laugh of guilty admission. 'I'll admit a soupçon of curiosity. I have only ever met one person with a butler. She was a client and she lived in an enormous manor house. I figured you for a quaint country cottage.'

Now it was my turn to laugh. I was the quaint country cottage kind of person. I just hadn't ended up living in one. He and I killed the next hour as we watched yet more people arrive and I told Tempest all about my adventure with the Maharaja and the house he gave me. Now that I was used to the idea of living in a giant manor house and having no bills, I found that I enjoyed telling the tale. Below us, two men were managing the gate to let cars in. The cars then vanished deeper into the plant and those which were visible at the front earlier were collected and also driven out of sight.

As the day began to wane, the number of people arriving dwindled, and in the past fifteen minutes no new cars had appeared. We had counted fifty-three cars in total. Assuming one passenger per car and allowing for there to have been only two people here before Mortice, then there were at least fifty-five people inside and the number could be four times that if the cars were full.

Tempest had a powerbar in his pocket that we shared. It was high in calories and carbohydrates he told me, the perfect thing to carry just in case it was necessary to miss a meal. It kept us ticking over, but now it was time to go.

Our plan was simple: We were going to find a break in the fence and let ourselves in. Then we were going to find the people and see what they were up to. It could be a giant waste of our time and we would discover it *was* a choral society we had snuck up on. We both doubted that though; the event had secret pagan cult etched all over it.

The meadow went right up to and through the fence, obscuring the bottom three feet of it. This made it harder to find a tear in the wire, but not impossible, Tempest finding one big enough for us to get through after just a few minutes.

Before we went through, I placed a call to Mike Atwell. 'Mike,' I said when he answered.

'Patricia, where are you? You shot off this morning.'

'Yes. Sorry about that.'

'That's fine. I had to leave a few minutes later myself. I got the weirdest call – a local internet entrepreneur found a headless animal in his bed.'

'Ewww. Like in the *Godfather*?' I asked, screwing my face up in disgust.

'Yeah. Except that was just the head and this was everything but. The victim is Ivor Biggun, the porn industry king.'

'Oh.' I had heard of him at least; his ridiculous fake name was one a person remembered if nothing else. 'Don't they call him the Hugh Heffner of the United Kingdom?'

'That's him,' Mike replied. 'He lives in Chislehurst in a ridiculous manor house called The Player's Mansion. It's so derivative. Anyway, I guess he upset someone, because he has a dead goat in his bed. He's getting all upset because he has a big seventieth birthday bash in a couple of days and wants this dealt with discreetly.'

Temporarily distracted by the headless animal story, I remembered what I called for. 'Mike, it might be nothing, but Tempest and I looked into the marks on Gerard Gallagher's shoulder and when we asked a supposed expert about them in Canterbury, he acted strangely and kicked us out of his shop. He got quite shirty actually, so we followed him to an abandoned industrial unit outside of Newington.'

'Newington?' Mike asked, the name unfamiliar.

'It's on the A2, just off the A249, but it's not very big. There is a gathering here and I am willing to bet they are up to no good. It might be the people responsible for the body in Upnor woods this morning, but equally, it might not be.' I gave him directions as best as I could, but he didn't sound very positive.

'I'm not sure how much cavalry I will be able to drum up. Chief Inspector Quinn is running this investigation now. After Gerard's body was found this morning, he assigned himself as lead officer. You know what a career man he is – he sees this case as high-profile so wants to solve it himself.'

'Can you make a call? There might be hundreds of them here. If it is the same group, then they killed a man last night and Tempest and I are walking into the lion's den.'

'I need proof to go to them with, Patricia. You know how many false leads they get to follow. Can you get some footage of them doing crazy pagan stuff? If they are clearly engaged in illegal or suspicious activities, I can guarantee a taskforce will descend on your location; assuming that is I can work out where you are. I'll make a call now and at least have Quinn put his team on alert.' I knew it was the best I could hope for. I thanked him and disconnected.

Tempest was waiting for me. 'No luck, huh?'

'Mike is a good guy, but he's not running the show and he doesn't have the ability to deploy armed officers.'

'No,' Tempest agreed. 'That falls to Chief Inspector Quinn. He and I do not see eye to eye generally. It's a good thing the call came from you. In fact, if Quinn knew it were me, he might just leave me hanging in the breeze to see if I survived. Regardless, they wouldn't get here before dark and we don't know for sure if there is anything of interest happening. I'm going to call a friend just in case.'

'A friend?'

'Yes. An old army buddy. He's useful when situations get tricky.' As Tempest sent a message, I called Jermaine.

'Good evening, madam.'

'Jermaine, are you busy?'

'I serve at your pleasure, madam. Whatever task you need me to perform is what I will find myself busy with.'

I should have known that would be his answer before I asked it. 'I might need your assistance. It's a John Steed situation.' I heard a very slight inrush of air as my butler got excited but did his very best to stifle it. Jermaine had bodyguard training as part of his butler duties; he was expected to be able to defend whichever principal he was appointed to, but his abilities went far beyond that. He also liked to dress as John Steed

35

from the Avengers, the original television series, not the comic book heroes now dominating the big screen. I gave him my location as best I could, checked that he had been able to collect Anna without problem, and let him go. He would be here as soon as he could. I knew that would be most of an hour though, so we were on our own until then.

Nevertheless, we were going in.

Tempest walked naturally as he made his way to the first building. We were crossing open ground and didn't want to look like we were trying to be surreptitious. Once he gained the shadows here, he went into stealth mode and I copied him, mirroring his movements as we sidled into the plant.

The first building was an enormous empty silo; the roof towered twenty yards above us. It had been picked clean inside; the guts of an overhead crane hung above us but the crane itself and everything else were long gone. We passed through it and out the other side as the sun continued toward the horizon and the shadows grew ever longer.

We heard talking at the same time as we saw the cars. It was one man's voice I decided. To me, it sounded like he was making a speech, his words emphatic, but every now and then he would pause, and a host of other voices would answer him. We couldn't make out his words yet; the sound was bouncing off the empty buildings to arrive as a confused jumble of echoes.

'We need to get closer,' I whispered as we peered around the corner of a building.

Tempest used two fingers to silently indicate where the sound was coming from. We couldn't see anyone from where we were, but a few yards further on, heads started to appear. In the centre of the plant was what I guessed to have originally been a drainage pool. Now empty of water, it created a natural amphitheatre and they were all in it. The dancing light from dozens of burning torches, held in the hands of the followers, lit the assembly. They were all in simple white robes with flowers in their hair and around their necks. Their faces were covered by eye masks, the kind a person wears to a masquerade ball though each

37

was white, and some had been adorned with more of the flower strings. To our right as we faced it, was the man they were all listening to.

He was a high priest, or whatever the correct name is for a pagan spiritual leader. He wore a purple cloak that fell to the floor and a fur stole over his shoulders that hung down his back. On his head, he wore a ram's skull complete with horns and a mask that obscured his face.

The high priest had his arms in the air as he preached to his audience, his voice loud enough to carry without need for amplification, and finally clear enough to hear. 'The moon is almost over the cusp of Orion. Tomorrow is the solstice of our new lord and we will bathe in the glory of Quentiox as he rises from his slumber to bestow us with his mighty power. We will all triumph as he breathes new life to this world. Through him we each of us will succeed in life and fulfil our dreams as our challengers fail in our wake.'

His audience responded. 'Bring us life anew in this barren land.'

As Tempest watched, I made my way back to the cars. I had spotted an open boot lid with something sticking out of it a moment ago. Now I knew what I had seen, so when I returned to Tempest a few seconds later, I had two robes in my hand and several strings of flowers. The flowers were fake, which struck me as ironic given the Earth mother nature of this religion.

Tempest saw them and immediately knew what I had in mind. 'Great idea.'

We donned the robes, adjusting each other's clothing until we looked the part. Tempest hung flowers in my hair, and I wound a string around his neck. Then, as the last rays of the sun slipped beneath the horizon, we joined the happy throng of pagan worshippers.

All the while we were hurriedly getting dressed, the high priest had continued to rant. He was building to something; the crowd being whipped into a frenzy by his words. It was all about gaining power and how they were going to flourish by helping an Earth god called Quentiox to rise. I really wanted to prod the person next to me and ask them what he was talking about but that would have given us away.

The high priest paused again and all around us the crowd murmured their response. Tempest and I both moved our lips, so it looked like we were taking part, but no one was paying us any attention. Tempest slipped through the row of people in front of us and we could then see that there were more rows, three or four deep, and our worst fears were realised as I did a head count to estimate that there were close to two-hundred followers here.

It *was* a cult.

That was the message hammering across my brain. Arguably more dangerous than many of the gangsters, thugs, and other criminals I had faced, cult members bore a fervour which eclipsed all sense of self-preservation.

I caught up to Tempest, lightly brushing my fingers against his to get his attention. 'What's our play?' I asked quietly, worried for what might happen to us if we were detected.

From the corner of his mouth, he whispered. 'We pull back and wait for the cavalry. There're too many of them for us to do anything ourselves. I'm going to contact Quinn though. He needs to send everyone he has right now.'

I couldn't agree more but before we could begin to fade backward through the crowd and escape, the high priest reached his grand finale.

39

'Loyal disciples of Quentiox, the time has come for us to give praise to our god. Bring forth the offering.'

Squeals and gasps of excitement reverberated around the amphitheatre just before the sound of a woman screeching in protest reached my ears. Beside me, Tempest stiffened and through the press of bodies we saw a young woman being dragged from the shadows behind the high priest.

Immediately alert, I focused on her face, trying to discern if it was Helena Gallagher, but I could instantly tell that it wasn't. This woman was too young, and her hair was much longer. She looked to be nineteen or twenty and beyond terrified as four large men dragged her before the crowd. Like everyone else, she wore a simple white robe but hers had been embroidered all over with symbols. Two women stepped forward to place garlands of flowers over her neck as she spat and swore and struggled for freedom.

People were surging forward, taking Tempest and me with them. He grabbed my hand, whispering a hushed but urgent message, 'Get to safety. Get back outside the perimeter and guide the police in if you get the chance to.'

'What are you going to do?' I gasped, terrified to leave him, horrified by what might be about to happen, and wanting for us both to leave. I knew we couldn't, though, not now that they had shown us their intended victim.

Tempest growled, 'Something dangerous.' Then he slipped away and was lost from sight as he wove through the throng of followers. I caught a glimpse of him once or twice, his short hair and trimmed beard the only thing I could use to identify him from the others.

He was going for the woman, that much was clear, but he needed a distraction. My stillness worked in my favour, the crowd passing me as they all pressed forward to see the sacrifice, since I was sure that was the woman's purpose. I hadn't seen an altar or a woven chair like poor Gerard had in the woods. However, when I got to the top of the bowl-like depression they were all in, and looked back down, I saw one of the men at the front produce a knife and hand it to the high priest. It glinted in the light cast by the fires, so I saw the wavy shape of the blade and knew it was the same one they used to kill Gerard just a few hours ago.

Ten yards away were rows of cars and I knew what I needed to do. Passing them earlier, we both saw the piles of clothes on the seats – the cult members were naked beneath their robes but what it meant to me now was that they couldn't have taken their car keys with them.

The first car I came to was a newish BMW seven series. An expensive car by anyone's standards. Carefully, I slipped inside, turned the key still hanging in the ignition, and stamped on the gas. It rocketed forward, picking up speed as I drove it into the amphitheatre, jumping out at the last moment as it crashed heavily into the steps of the concrete bowl. The crowd were at the other end so there was no danger to life, but it did the trick. I bruised my shoulder and whacked my head on the rough ground but there was no time to rub my injuries because I had everyone's attention, two hundred sets of eyes swinging my way.

Tempest took it as his cue to act. From above them all I had a perfect view as he smashed an elbow into the man next to him and tore across the ground to reach the men holding the still-screaming victim. With their hands occupied, they couldn't stop him as he leapt to kick the nearest, his spinning foot striking the man on his chin.

As the man was flung backward, he let go of the girl but not soon enough to prevent her from being pulled after him which worked for

Tempest as it left the man holding her other arm with empty hands and a surprised expression. A hard punch to his jaw felled him but I didn't get to see anything else because the enraged crowd were surging. Half of them were converging on Tempest and half on my position.

Terror made my feet move, quick steps carrying me to the next nearest car, this time a large Ford utility truck. I dove inside, but the keys weren't in it. I shot my eyes to look out of the windscreen which was a mistake because what I saw induced a bout of panic that made me feel dizzy. A horde was coming over the rim of the bowl and they were running in my direction. Even with the masks on, I could see the fury in their eyes.

With my fingers scrambling, I dug for the keys in the pile of man's clothing I found on the driver's seat. They had to be in one of his trouser pockets. They weren't though, and my chance to try a different car was lost as the pagans closed the distance to me. A squeal of fright escaped my lips as the doors were yanked open from both sides. I kicked and slapped at the hands that came in to grab me; ultimately, there were too many of them and I was pulled from the car with multiple hands on each limb as they bore me aloft and back to the bowl.

Going feet first, I had to lift my head, one of the few things not being held, when I heard Tempest's voice ring out.

'One more move, and the woman dies!' he bellowed.

Peering between my feet, I could see him on the far side of the makeshift amphitheatre. There were cult members to his left and right but no one behind him. Half a dozen men were being picked up where he had knocked them down but to my surprise, he was now holding the woman in her ceremonial robe and had the knife pressed to her throat.

42

The high priest was being helped back to his feet; Tempest must have tackled him to get the knife.

'What are you going to do, non-believer? Sacrifice the woman we were going to sacrifice?' the high priest chuckled. 'Hardly a threat that will scare us.'

Constantly checking to his left and right to judge who was going to attack first, Tempest didn't look at the high priest when he answered. 'You are right that I am a non-believer. What would it mean to Quentiox if she were to be killed by my hand? Would he recognise your tribute?'

The woman squealed in pain as Tempest made a show of pushing the knife harder into her jugular. The high priest waved his hands to stop the men advancing – Tempest had bought some time.

'Good. Your men over there have my partner. Tell them to put her down nice and gently.'

As if seeing me for the first time, the high priest looked my way but shook his head. 'No, I don't think so. I think you have granted me a stalemate that only I can win. You will hand over the woman or I will have my loyal followers rip your partner limb from limb.'

I didn't like the sound of that, and I really didn't like the hands tightening around my arms and legs as they prepared to obey the command.

An explosion ripped through the air, the flash of blinding light and thunderous roar came from behind Tempest, illuminating him and casting him as a silhouette simultaneously. I only caught a glimpse as he stood tall when everyone else cringed away, then the hands that held me aloft began to let go and I tumbled to the ground as a helicopter flew over the top of the huge empty silo.

Its search light flashed on just before the loudspeaker began shouting instructions. Pinned in the beam of light, the cult scattered.

Overhead, a familiar voice rang out, 'Everyone stay where you are. This is the police. You are surrounded and will be fired upon if you attempt to flee.' Mike was here! Mike was here with the cavalry and they were going to capture all of them. All Tempest and I had to do was stay out of harm's way for a few more seconds.

However, the armed officers I expected to swarm the area, with their assault rifles at the ready, failed to appear. Unimpeded, the cult members were running to their cars and peeling out of the plant with screeching tyres and beeping horns. More noise came from the sound of several crashes as panicked drivers bumped one another in their haste to get away.

The high priest was being helped to a waiting car, the door held open to get him inside, and I saw the indecision on Tempest's face as he held the woman, much more gently now, and argued with himself about leaving her to catch the high priest. If he caught him, this might all be over, but how could he push the traumatised woman away when she clung to him so desperately? His indecision made the decision for him as the doors slammed shut and the car pelted from the scene. The helicopter's search light tried to follow it, but I knew the cars would find their way to the canopy of trees just outside the plant and could then vanish from sight.

Where were the armed response team Mike shouted about?

The dust was beginning to settle in the space between the buildings as I painfully clawed my way back onto my feet. In the space of less than two minutes, the two hundred followers had all escaped, none of them were left for us to question. We had rescued a woman though; rescued her from certain death I thought. We also had someone's car; the crashed BMW stuck in the bottom of the drainage pool where it would require a crane to get it out. It would be easy enough to trace its owner, so they might have escaped, but we would be hot on their heels. The police too.

I crossed to Tempest, meaning to give some comfort to the young woman but was stopped short when a shadow emerged from the building behind Tempest. This was our chance to capture one of them!

'Tempest, there's one behind you! I've got the girl.' I meant to look after her as he, the far more capable, stronger, and well-trained man tackled the man coming out of the darkness. Tempest said something to the woman as he detached himself from her and turned to face the last remaining cult member. Then he paused and I saw why – the man he needed to tackle was huge. He had to be over six and half feet tall and wide enough across his shoulders to make Tempest look small.

Nevertheless, Tempest's hesitancy surprised me; I expected him to attack the man no matter what. A few minutes ago, he had taken on two hundred of them as he raced to get to the woman.

The big man kept coming forward, stepping out of the shadow cast by the building so that I saw the incongruity – he was dressed more like batman than a cult member. Where he ought to have on a flowing white robe and flowers, he had combat trousers and a Kevlar vest.

'Was the explosion big enough?' he asked, just before Tempest high-fived him.

Then a shout from behind me brought my head around to see Barbie running toward me. She looked to have come directly from the gym, her body clad in form-fitting Lycra which showed all her bumps and curves.

Having turned around, the large man in the Kevlar vest was now behind me, but I heard him say, 'Stand back, Tempest. I have radar lock on my next target, and I am going in for the kill.' I wasn't certain what he meant by his comment, but I had a pretty good idea that he was eyeing up my young blonde friend as if she were a tasty morsel.

The helicopter had landed beyond the main entrance to the abandoned plant. I heard it touch down just before I saw the tall man

46

appear behind Tempest, so it was no surprise when I saw Jermaine and Detective Sergeant Mike Atwell emerge from the darkness just as Barbie had.

Barbie reached me. 'Patty! Oh, my gosh. I'm so glad you are alright. Jermaine said you were doing something ridiculously brave again. Is everyone alright? Who are those two men? Is one of them the Tempest guy you told me about?' Her mouth was running ten to the dozen again, a sure sign that she was fuelled by adrenalin right now. So too was her constant movement; she could barely keep still.

I had a question that overruled hers though. 'Where did you get a helicopter?'

'That was my doing, madam,' admitted Jermaine, arriving with Mike Atwell just as Tempest got to us with the young woman and the man in the Kevlar vest.

I had lots of questions for my friends, but the almost-sacrifice had to take priority, the sound of distant sirens promising more help as we made sure the poor girl knew she was safe. She still clung to Tempest as if he were a rock in a storm, but she was able to speak so we took her to the helicopter where she could sit comfortably and asked her a thousand questions.

Her name was Linda Cole, she was a beauty therapist from Swanley and had been grabbed outside her door three days ago as she came home from a date. They hadn't hurt her, but there was plenty of threat that they would, should she attempt to escape or in any way disobey them. They never showed their faces, but they all spoke with local accents and they were all Caucasians.

She hadn't met or even seen the high priest before this evening and had no idea what they had planned for her though she knew it was

47

nothing good. She had been kept in a lockup and transported blindfolded, the cult members cautious to a fault, but she told us there were other captives.

'Did you learn any names?' I asked, hoping she would be able to tell me Helena Gallagher was still alive.

Quietly, she said, 'Yes. There were six of us. Helena said she had been there for more than a week when I arrived. I never saw any of them but when we were unguarded, we could talk so we got to learn lots about each other.' She gave us a list of names, all of whom Mike confirmed had been reported as missing at some point in the last few days.

Taking Tempest to one side as Mike continued to ask questions, I said, 'The high priest said the event is tomorrow.'

'Yes,' Tempest agreed. 'He called it the solstice of their new lord, though I think he has his terminology confused. A solstice is when the sun reaches the most northern or southern point from the equator. However, that is semantics. He is planning some big event tomorrow night and I don't know if what we did tonight will stop that from occurring. I think it unlikely.'

I had to agree. 'We have a ticking clock to work out who they are and where they will be and figure out how to stop them.'

'Easy then,' joked Tempest though we both knew how grave the situation was for the women held captive.

I noticed Jermaine was chatting with the tall man wearing Kevlar. He was tall enough that he even made Jermaine look a little short. 'Who is that?' I asked.

Tempest started toward them, walking backward so he could speak to me. 'I think some introductions are in order. I also want to hear where the helicopter came from.'

'I guess you two have met,' I said as I approached the two tall men. Jermaine addressed me. 'Madam, this is Big Ben Winters.'

'Hey, babe,' Big Ben said with a cheeky wink. 'You can call me Big Ben. Is your blonde friend married, spoken for, otherwise unavailable for nocturnal activities?'

His forwardness was surprising.

Tempest admonished him. 'Knock it off, Ben. Bigger fish to fry right now.'

Big Ben wasn't to be dissuaded from his interest in Barbie that easily though. 'Don't worry, short stuff,' he chuckled. 'I'm just getting things ready for the victory party after we catch everyone and make them hurt.'

I shook my head to clear it, but Jermaine answered his question first. 'Miss Berkeley is dating a doctor at St Barts hospital. I am afraid she is very much spoken for.'

Big Ben waggled his eyebrows. 'We'll see. Big Ben can play the long game.'

Internally I had to admit I wanted to know why he called himself Big Ben but given his demeanour, I doubted I would like the answer. In fact, I expected it to be something rude.

Tempest jumped in with a question, reaching out with one hand to tap the helicopter. 'So how did you come by the bird?'

Jermaine was about to speak when Barbie stuck her head out of the helicopter to say, 'Jermaine is dating the pilot.'

I looked at Jermaine, who now looked embarrassed though there was no need to be. I glanced inside where the pilot still wore his headset and was checking over his gauges and instruments. He was a good-looking man in his late twenties, a little like Tempest in his facial features and facial hair.

Jermaine said, 'When you called to give me your location and a brief rundown on what you were intending to do, I knew you would be placing yourself in danger.'

'Hold on,' I protested. 'I never mentioned that I was doing anything even remotely dangerous.'

A smile flickered across Jermaine's face. Barbie leaned out of the helicopter again. 'That's how we knew we needed to get here quickly. When you downplay it, it is always some deadly game of cat and mouse you have got into.'

Jermaine cleared his throat. 'Yes. Well, I thought haste might be prudent but knowing you were with Mr Michaels, I chose to call the Blue Moon office. I spoke with a young lady called Jane Butterworth and she put me in contact with Mr Winters. I also contacted Detective Sergeant Atwell and arranged for us all to meet at Rochester airport where Marcus kindly had his helicopter waiting.'

'They dropped me short so the rotor noise wouldn't give the game away,' added Big Ben, picking up the story. 'They gave me ten minutes and waited for me to blow some stuff up.'

'What did you find to blow up?' I asked, wondering if I should ask such a question in hearing distance of a serving police officer.

Big Ben smiled. 'It doesn't take much. That was a can of gasoline, a car battery, and some wire. It's not the sort of thing I would advise kids to try at home, but it came in handy in places like Iraq.'

The wail of sirens was getting closer, the lights from them appearing like strobes through small gaps in the canopy of trees on the A2 road through Newington. In a couple of minutes, they would arrive, and poor Linda would have yet more questions to answer. She was safe, and that was the important thing. The procession of flashing lights would have an ambulance with them I felt sure, so with nothing left that I could do for the victim, I wanted to go back and inspect the amphitheatre again.

We all went. All except Mike, who felt it his duty to remain with Linda until he could hand her over to the paramedics. The five of us formed a straight line, walking back toward the bowl in the centre of the plant, each using the light on our phones to illuminate the ground in front of us. Anything could be a clue at this point. Mike had already sent the registration number from the BMW I crashed back to his headquarters; they would have an answer for who owned it shortly and that would give the police someone to arrest.

There might be more though, and we were scouring the ground for whatever there might be to find. A wallet would be nice, especially if it contained someone's identification and the address for the lockup where the women were being kept. Two minutes later, when the sirens started to shut off, and it was obvious the police had finally arrived, we had turned up nothing whatsoever. No dropped business cards, no crumpled notes. Tempest and Big Ben were just about to start taking the car apart when a dozen pairs of heavy footsteps came running in our direction. They echoed as they ran through the silo before emerging into the moonlight on our side. A man with a loud hailer started barking orders.

'All of you, step away from the crime scene. You are now interfering with a police investigation and will be arrested if you persist.'

I frowned deeply. The man with the loudspeaker was Chief Inspector Quinn. We had met several times, and on each occasion, he had treated me with respect and dignity and presented himself as a decent man. I knew Mike to have a less than complimentary opinion, though, and Tempest appeared to almost loathe the man, but this was my first negative encounter and I was going to speak with him.

52

'Chief Inspector,' I called as I crossed the ground to get to him. 'Chief Inspector, it's Patricia Fisher.'

He finished giving instruction to a uniformed sergeant before turning his attention my way. 'Yes, Mrs Fisher, I was informed that you were here. Now I need you to take your colleagues and move out of the way. It is time for the professionals to take over.'

I was incensed by his attitude. 'Chief Inspector, were it not for the people you are so gleefully kicking out of this crime scene, you wouldn't even know it was one.'

Tempest joined me, Big Ben on his shoulder. 'Yes, Quinny,' said Tempest. 'What ever would you do without us?'

I thought for a moment that the senior police officer was going to start shouting but he smiled instead. 'Mr Michaels, I tolerate you only because you get results. Regardless of that, and regardless of the fact that Miss Cole will tell the press you saved her from certain death, I must insist that you respect the need for my officers to now take over this investigation. If we are to arrest and prosecute, the correct chain of evidence must be observed.'

It was a calm and rational argument against which neither Tempest nor I nor anyone else could possibly hope to fight. Had he led with that argument I would have respectfully withdrawn, now I had no choice but to do so and the chief inspector had scored a point; something Mike Atwell had warned me he liked to do.

We were essentially dismissed, CI Quinn choosing to move around us to bark another order at new officers just arriving. We were just about to move away when the sound of another helicopter pierced the night sky.

'Reporters,' murmured Tempest, his comment causing Big Ben to produce a mirror from a pocket on his Kevlar vest. He used it to check his hair and teeth before dropping to the floor to do some press ups. When he jumped back up to check the veins on his biceps, Tempest said, 'He knows that the television stations pick attractive women to put in front of the camera. Statistically, over seventy percent of on the ground reporters are now women and they all fall inside a very small demographic; twenty-eight to thirty-five, five feet eight to five ten and almost always brunette.'

'How on Earth do you know that,' I had to ask.

Tempest pointed at Big Ben. 'He likes to study his enemy.'

The helicopter came closer and swung around to show that it wasn't a news crew at all. Big Ben deflated, moaning something about hitting town when he got home and started walking back to the helicopter he arrived in. Tempest and I followed him, with Barbie and Jermaine having already been shooed away by the police so we were all there when the chief inspector dashed by us to greet the new arrivals. The rotors were beating the foliage into submission and kicking up dust from the dry summer. The pilot shut down the engine; clearly, they were planning to stay a while, and two men got out.

I recognised one of them though I couldn't immediately say where from or who he was. He was athletic looking, though in his early sixties and possessed a vibrancy I rarely saw in men that age. He reminded me a lot of Alistair Huntley, the captain of the Aurelia, the cruise ship aboard which I travelled the world. Beside him, and looking angry, was a short police officer in uniform. I could tell by the amount of braiding on his jacket that he had to be someone senior. Beneath his hat, which he held in place as he hurried away from the helicopter, was grey hair going white. He had a pointy nose and small ears which made his head look a bit like a turnip. Once both men were clear of the blades, they stood up and I got to see that the man in uniform really was quite short. Five feet and five inches perhaps. I didn't recognise him at all, but Tempest did.

'That's Albert Brady, the Chief Constable for Kent,' he told me.

'Who's the man in the suit,' I asked.

Tempest seemed surprised by my question. 'That's the Lord Mayor of Kent. Did you miss the big news event ... yes, of course you did. That would have been when you were on your cruise. His name is David Sebastian. The big idea is that each County across England and Wales will now have a Lord Mayor who oversees all the city mayors. Quite what difference that will make to the citizens I have no idea, but there were six candidates and this chap won by a giant landslide.'

'What's he doing here?' I wanted to know.

Tempest blew out a breath through his nose, muttering, 'I have no idea.'

The chief inspector went to meet them both, the sound of his voice carrying as he shouted to be heard above the helicopter's engine. As he greeted them, the chief constable started speaking.

'Who authorised the deployment of so many of my troops, Chief Inspector?' His tone was surly and disapproving.

The chief inspector looked to be momentarily lost for words. 'I authorised it, sir.'

The chief constable nodded as if he already knew the answer before he asked it but wanted the admission of guilt from the man himself. 'And what, pray, do you feel justified such an overindulged response? What other crimes are being committed when you have so many of my officers here? What do you believe the cost of such a deployment is? The lord mayor here is cracking down on exactly this kind of flagrant misuse of police resources. Your hair trigger cost the County hundreds of thousands of pounds tonight. I don't see anyone in cuffs, Chief Inspector. Where are my criminals?'

Bewilderment fighting with shock and embarrassment fought to dominate Chief Inspector Quinn's face as everyone watched him being torn apart. 'Sir, I responded to a call which made me believe the recent spate of missing persons may be at the hands of a pagan cult. Civilians at the scene had discovered a woman being held against her will and were attempting a rescue. At the time of dispatch, I had no way of knowing if the rescue attempt would be successful or how many cult members we might face. Arriving short-handed could have endangered the lives of the officers responding and resulted in a worse situation.'

'A cunning answer,' the chief constable snapped. 'What evidence is there that such a cult even exists, man? I have seen no evidence of a murderous pagan cult operating in Kent, and I can assure you, as chief constable, I am far better informed than you are. Show me a single scrap of evidence that this wasn't a complete waste of time and resources.'

As the chief constable continued to rant, the lord mayor had taken it upon himself to mingle with the police officers. He was doing the rounds, shaking hands and being a politician. He had an easy smile I noticed, and I surprised myself when he turned his attention my way and my stomach gave a small flutter. His eyes lit up as if he recognised me. I was sure I didn't look my best; rotor wash, bits of flying dirt and diving out of cars hadn't left me in a glamorous state but he was making a beeline for me now regardless.

Chief Inspector Quinn continued to argue with his superior. 'What about Linda Cole, sir? She reported over two hundred cult members here. A number corroborated by the civilians at the scene who rescued her. She claims there are several other women still held captive and the cult may be planning a mass sacrifice tomorrow. Her testimony should be enough to mobilize a task force, sir.'

The lord mayor extended his hand to me. 'Mrs Patricia Fisher, famous saviour of Zangrabar and now a licensed detective I understand. What an honour it is to meet you.'

'Um.' It was all I could think of to say. I couldn't imagine why anyone would think it an honour to meet me, but I found myself a little mesmerised by the handsome man, as if his presence filled all the available space leaving no room for my words. He was my height and he sure was nice to look at. His hand was soft yet masculine as it kept hold of mine so he could stare into my eyes. Barbie nudged me. 'Yes, hello,' I managed to blurt. 'Nice to, um, meet. Is it hot suddenly?' I asked Barbie. She rolled her eyes.

The lord mayor still hadn't released my hand as he continued to praise me, 'I believe it was your detective work that led to Mrs Cole being rescued this evening. Sterling work I am sure.'

Finding my voice, I said, 'It was a joint effort between Tempest Michaels and me though the greater team had to join in to achieve the partial victory.' I used my hand to indicate Barbie, Jermaine, and Big Ben.

'Partial victory?' he questioned. 'I should say it was an unbridled triumph. Well done one and all.' He made a big show of pumping even more arms as he congratulated everyone personally with a lord mayor's handshake.

I tried to explain a little more clearly. 'What I mean is. We were successful in recovering Linda, but the cult members all escaped. We have a few leads, but they are still out there with several women who I am sure they plan to kill tomorrow. Actually,' the urgency of the situation chimed inside my head, 'we really ought to be getting on with it. The clock is ticking.'

He held up both hands in a 'whoa' gesture. 'Surely this is a job for the police now. That is why I insisted the chief constable accompany me himself. He will set the matter straight and get the best people working on it.' He beckoned the chief constable. 'Albert, please tell these wonderful people that they can relax now. The police may have been slow off the mark this time, but they have the resources and the manpower to bring about a swift conclusion. Isn't that right?'

The chief constable eyed us warily as if we were somehow the problem. 'Well-meaning. That is how I see you. Spirited too, but I cannot allow you to further interfere with such a delicate and sensitive case. Failing now could have terrible political ramifications for the lord mayor. You should not have been here in the first place. That you rescued a woman notwithstanding,' he added quickly as he saw Tempest's face turn to a scowl and a protest forming on his lips. 'My officers will escort you from the scene.'

'We have a helicopter, big boy,' said Big Ben with a sneer. 'Do the police have a helicopter? Just, you know, since you are bragging about how well resourced you are.'

The chief constable narrowed his eyes but didn't respond to the goading. Instead, he turned his head slightly to speak to Chief Inspector Quinn who was silently fuming just behind the senior officer. 'Quinn, you said one of your officers accompanied these civilians to the scene and alerted you to the presence of the cult here tonight?'

Mike Atwell heard the question and stepped forward. 'Indeed, sir. That was me. I received a call from Mrs F ...'

'Yes, yes. I don't recall asking for a life history man,' snapped the chief constable. Focusing on Quinn he said, 'This is precisely the reason why you remain a chief inspector, Quinn. You have no knowledge of the activities of your own men and allow them to think they can circumvent the chain of command to galivant around in a helicopter, charging to the rescue like John Wayne.' I don't think any of us could believe what we were hearing, but he wasn't finished yet. Swinging his head back around to look straight at my friend, Detective Sergeant Mike Atwell, he said, 'You're fired. Effective immediately. You can leave your identification here.'

Outraged, I gasped, but Mike was already arguing. 'You can't do that. What about due process?'

The chief constable chuckled. 'A formality. I'm the chief constable, you idiot. You can have your hearing in two days' time and then it will be official.' Then he started walking away, heading back to the helicopter. As he passed CI Quinn, he growled, 'Make sure he leaves his ID with you and get these civilians out of here.'

Meekly, Quinn said, 'Yes, sir,' his eyes unable to meet any of ours.

The lord mayor took a pace backwards, his face betraying how awkward the situation now felt for everyone. 'Patricia, it was lovely to meet you. I hope we can get together socially some time. I'll have my people set something up.' Then he too was gone, jogging to the helicopter before I could respond. As he went away from us, I noticed something that seemed out of place with his perfectly manicured appearance: he had hat hair; a line around the back of his head where something had indented his hair.

Behind me, Barbie said, 'Wow, that was horrible.'

I nodded. I felt close to speechless, but I managed to mutter, 'I need a gin.'

Clues

My car was in the village a mile and half away, Tempest's car was back at the office in Rochester and all any of us wanted to do was retire somewhere to drown our sorrows. Never before had I seen a victory turn so swiftly sour. Mike was quiet on the flight home, the decision to abandon the cars and just head to my house one to which everyone agreed.

Marcus happily flew us directly to my house where he planned to park on the lawn. He knew where my house was and that his helicopter would fit because, apparently, he had been visiting with Jermaine for some time. On the way, Tempest pulled out his phone saying, 'I need to make some calls. I ought to let my partner, Amanda, know I will be late, but I think we need to talk to Frank again. He will be able to provide us with information on Quentiox. It may prove pertinent. It may not. He's the guy for it though.'

While Tempest made calls, pausing only to confirm my address, I called Helena's father, Jerry Brock. He begged me for good news, which I could not give him, and I was careful to not overstate what I knew. We had rescued a woman this evening, but his daughter hadn't been there. The rescued woman had claimed his daughter was still alive, though, and that was some small comfort. I kept the detail brief because I really didn't know much and promised, not for the first time, that I was working on nothing other than trying to retrieve his daughter. Once I ended the call to my client, I talked the case through with Mike, trying to keep his mind off recent events. I already knew I was going to offer him a job. I felt terrible that he had been fired and would soon have no income. However, I knew he was a capable detective so, if he agreed to it, he would work with me. I certainly had enough cases to keep the pair of us occupied.

'Where do you think they are hiding the women?' I asked him. I knew it was a silly question because there was no way of knowing but if he was talking, then he wasn't miring in the depths of worry for his future.

He shrugged, pulling his eyes up to meet mine. 'It would need to be somewhere that is not frequented by other people. It couldn't be any old public-use lockup because someone would hear or see something. It also needs running water and a toilet; Linda said she was fed and looked after.'

'Will you be able to get access to talk to her again?' I asked.

He gave a definite shake of his head. 'Not a chance. Chief Inspector Quinn might have got some harsh treatment today, I can't say what got into the chief constable, but Quinn won't go against him. I won't get my police warrant back. I might not even bother with the hearing.'

I didn't argue with him, but it was a blow that we couldn't ask Linda more questions. There just hadn't been time to learn what she knew, and she was in quite a state when we rescued her so none of us pushed her for answers; it just wouldn't have been fair.

Barbie said, 'We can look up who owned the BMW you crashed. I can do that when we get home, then at least we will know who owns it and can pay them a visit.'

Mike shook his head again. 'I doubt they will be at home. If they were there tonight then they will know the police will be coming for them, or they will claim it was stolen and lawyer up so they don't have to say anything. Plus, if Quinn catches wind of any of us sticking our noses in, he will not hesitate to arrest us.'

'He can crack on,' laughed Big Ben. 'It wouldn't be the first time he arrested me. Tempest and I tend to do whatever is necessary and never concern ourselves with what the likes of Quinny might think.'

I said, 'I really thought we would find more clues tonight. I feel like we touched them but got nothing from it. Not so much as a fingerprint.'

Tempest chose that moment to end his call and held up a finger to get my attention. 'On the subject of evidence and clues ...' he pulled the ceremonial dagger from his inner jacket pocket. It was in a clear plastic bag. 'I forgot to mention that I had this.'

Mike Atwell's face became a frown. 'Hey, that's important evidence. The police should have that.'

He reached for it, but Tempest snatched it away. 'Dude, seriously? They just fired your arse. For doing your job, I might add. You're with us now, or you are on your own, but you are not with the police.' He held it up again so everyone could see it.

'It's really fancy,' observed Barbie. What does the wobbly blade add? Wibbly, wavy, I don't know what the right word is.'

'It's called Kris-style, but it adds nothing,' Tempest assured her. 'Actually, it makes it hard to use as a weapon because you cannot pull it out easily afterwards. It is designed to look attractive, so gullible idiots buy them. It smells though.'

'Smells?' asked Mike.

Tempest nodded. 'I noticed it as I was putting it in the bag. I had to seal the Ziplock with my teeth. It's a chemical smell of some sort. I think it might be worth having it analysed.'

Mike pulled out his phone. 'Well, that is something I probably can help with. Let's see how much credit I still have at the crime lab.'

While he made his mysterious call, I took the knife in its bag from Tempest and got my first good look at it. It was very possibly the weapon used to murder Gerard Gallagher a day ago. I felt a change in motion and glanced out of my window to see my house. Marcus was banking and descending.

Big Ben whistled. I almost did the same myself. I had seen the grand beauty at night before but seeing it from the air gave it a new perspective, somehow making it even bigger and more imposing.

Marcus touched down lightly, kissing the grass with his wheels as he settled the aircraft and began shutting it down. I had yet to speak to the man who had so generously come to our aid. I was sure he needed to be paid for the fuel and hire but that could be worked out later. Right now, I had an empty belly and an empty right hand where a cold glass of gin was supposed to be.

Breakfast

In the morning, there were a lot of us for breakfast, and I liked having the house full for a change. We had stayed up for an hour, talking through the case and examining the few clues we had unearthed. Then we made plans for today because we needed to get a number of things done quickly. To start with we needed to retrieve my car, but I found out, when I brought the subject up, that Jermaine had dispatched Tom the handyman first thing this morning. Quite how he was recovering it by himself I didn't ask. Mostly, I hoped it wasn't vandalised or otherwise damaged.

Tempest needed to get his car and Big Ben needed clothes as there was nothing in our house that fit him. I offered to have everyone taken home last night but people were tired and, I think, curious about the house so they wanted to stay.

'What's that glorious smell?' asked Big Ben arriving in the formal dining room where Mrs Ellis, the cook, had instructed Molly, the housemaid and cleaner, to set up. Before anyone could answer, he sniffed deeply again, and then announced, 'Ha! It's me. I smell great this morning.'

Barbie giggled at him, which got some side eye from Hideki. Last night Big Ben had been wearing black makeup to distort his face; the look went with the combat boots and Kevlar vest. However, this morning, with his hair arranged neatly and his skin fresh from the shower, even I had to admit that he was ridiculously handsome. Far too young for me but one couldn't deny that he had been put together well. Not that I thought Barbie's attention would be swayed, but Big Ben winked at her just as her boyfriend Hideki stood up, announcing he had to get going. He had a forty-hour shift to start at St Barts and his train left in twenty minutes.

Barbie met Hideki in Tokyo a little more than three months ago when the cruise ship docked there. He was working as a taxi driver to help pay his tuition fees and had helped us immensely while we were there, putting himself on the line to save us from Japanese criminals more than once. It had worked out for him as he was now dating my rather lovely blonde friend. Circumstance had pushed their relationship forward more swiftly than they might have wanted, but it was working out so far.

He and Barbie kissed, and he departed, which left the team from last night sitting around the table. Well, it almost did. I swivelled around in my chair to face Jermaine. He was standing almost to attention two yards behind me as if waiting for his next instruction. He must have risen early this morning, which was standard practice for him, but while the rest of us were in casual attire, he wore his full butler's livery with tails and a tie.

'Jermaine, will you please join us?'

'Madam?'

'Please. I know you love the formality of your role, but we have just a couple of days to solve this case and you are a part of that. I need … we all need Jermaine the ninja right now.'

'Yeah, big man, come join us,' agreed Big Ben.

As if resigning himself to his fate, he strode to a small closet in the corner of the room. I had never noticed it before; it wasn't a room I came into very often. There, he reached in to retrieve a hanger for his long, formal jacket. Then took a seat between Barbie and Tempest, selecting several pieces of fruit from the platter in the centre of the table.

Once settled, he asked, 'What is your plan for the day, madam?'

I looked at Tempest. 'Frank is coming here, yes?'

Tempest shot his cuff to check his watch. '0700hrs. He should be along shortly. He wants to get back to Rochester to open up at 0900hrs so I think he will be here quite soon.'

'Who is Frank?' asked Barbie as she tucked into a plate of eggs, smoked salmon, and avocado.

Tempest answered. 'He owns a bookshop in Rochester, but he is a local expert on everything weird and has always proved to be a limitless source of knowledge. I asked him about Quentiox last night, and I had to wake him up to do it. Even half asleep he started telling me all about him. He's some kind of goat-headed pagan god. Anyway, he'll be here soon and will probably bring a ton of research books with him.'

Mike chirped up, 'I spoke with two guys I know in the crime lab last night. You met them already, in fact. Simon and Steven?' I nodded.

Tempest said, 'I know them too. Through my business partner, Amanda. Are you going to have them analyse the dagger?'

Mike wiped a blob of egg from his lips with a napkin. 'Yes. I can't go there myself though. It will need to be someone else.'

Big Ben put his hand up to volunteer but got a sardonic look from Tempest. 'Put your hand down, you big doofus. All the cops met you. All the female cops especially, and you don't exactly blend in.'

Big Ben acknowledged the point, but said, 'I was going to suggest I call Patience Woods.'

'Patience?' questioned Barbie. 'Cute girl, caramel skin, and a whole lot of sass?'

Big Ben and Tempest both raised an eyebrow. 'That is one way to describe her,' said Tempest. 'You obviously met her at some point. The two ladies may draw the least attention if they go.'

Mike nodded. 'They offered to come here, but it will require the equipment in their lab to give us an answer.'

'So, we're going?' asked Barbie.

I said, 'Yup. You and me. Girl power.' We fist bumped. 'Then there is Mortice Keys, the man we followed to Newington.'

'That's right,' Tempest agreed. 'He vanished, but he has to have gone somewhere. Mike, do you think Quinn will use the information we gave him and police resources to find his car?'

'Absolutely. Chief Inspector Quinn might be a lot of things, but he is a professional policeman and he gives his all to solve every crime. He'll follow every lead he has. They will have identified the owner of the BMW Patricia crashed too.'

'Anthony Perkins,' supplied Barbie. When Mike looked surprised, she added, 'Sorry, I thought you knew. Jermaine and I looked that up last night. We have an address for him too.'

Mike looked flabbergasted. 'Why didn't you say anything? The police will want that information.'

'Don't they have their own database?' asked Jermaine.

Mike's cheeks coloured. 'Of course, sorry. I'm feeling a little off balance this morning.' Getting fired last night had thrown him a loop and I was yet to discuss my plan to employ him as a fellow detective. I didn't feel like the time was right yet, his wound was too raw so it would be like I

68

was a shark picking on a bleeding bather, getting him to agree to work with me when he was feeling weak. Recovering, he asked, 'So who is he?'

Barbie answered. 'A local businessman. Quite successful too. He runs a firm which makes stairlifts and small elevators, but his reported turnover in the last two quarters was four times what it was last year.'

'Big Ben and I can take him; we don't have a task yet.'

'Then I will return to Canterbury, madam,' Jermaine volunteered. 'If Mr Keys returns, I will call.'

The tasks had been divided up and we each had a job to be getting on with. Breakfast was done, and the sound of the doorbell echoing through the house told me Frank Decaux had most likely arrived.

Barbie bounced to her feet. 'I need to change,' she announced. Gym gear is not the thing for being unnoticed in a police station. 'Do we need to charm these guys or are they cool?'

Mike looked at her, unsure what she was asking. I understood though; she was asking how much cleavage would be required.

'They are cool, Barbie. No skin needed.'

I got a beaming smile in response. 'Cool.' Then, she followed Jermaine from the room, bounding after him as if her legs were made of springs.

Just as she left, my phone beeped with an incoming email. I saw who it was from and swiped my screen to read it. Angelica Howard-Box had sent me a message.

Patricia,

Due to your unacceptable and disruptive behaviour at your very first meeting, you are hereby dismissed from the church council. Under no circumstances are you to attend the meeting tonight. If you wish to appeal your dismissal, please do so in writing to the president of the church council.

Yours

Angelica Howard-Box

President of the Church Council

There was a part of me that really admired Angelica's ability to be an utter cow all of the time. I closed the message, acknowledging firstly that I didn't give two hoots what Angelica said, and secondly that I had more pressing concerns right now.

Old Books

Jermaine put his tails back on to answer the door, making sure Frank got the full effect. As usual, when I left the dining room to greet him, the new arrival was glancing about and looking startled because the house is, quite frankly, startling.

'Hello again, Frank.' My call got his attention, a smile splitting his face as he swung around to see who had spoken.

Tempest hallooed him as well.

Big Ben said, 'Morning, crazy pants. Have you got so many books in the car that you couldn't carry them?'

Frank blinked twice, but his smile never faltered. 'I do, as a matter of fact. Can I get a hand?'

All four men went out to Frank's car, a chocolate-brown Rover 400, returning moments later with an armful of books each. Frank had loose leaves of paper sticking out from his pile; they looked to be printed pages from the internet, but he was gushing with excitement as he tottered along beneath his load.

'I was up most of the night making calls and cross referencing what I found. It might just be that we are about to witness a fully entropic crossover of cataclysmic proportions.'

I had to eye him cautiously, remembering Tempest's advice that it was good to listen but rarely worth heeding ninety percent of what Frank said. I led them to my office at the back of the house where Anna was to be found in a basket. Her puppies were there too, all five dogs choosing to bounce from their beds to attack the guests.

71

'Wow,' said Tempest. 'I haven't seen a dachshund puppy since I got mine from the breeder. I forgot how small they are.' John, Paul, Georgie, and Ringo recognised a sucker when they spotted one getting on the floor and were soon all climbing him. Anna, who slept in a separate bed, went to Big Ben, but gave Frank an experimental sniff on her way. She met Big Ben last night and was instantly smitten by him. He made a comment about women finding him irresistible regardless of breed or race which elicited an eye roll from Tempest. I simply ignored him.

Frank wasted no time, selecting a huge tome, bound in what appeared to be alligator skin with a large clasp that required a key to open it. He turned the book so that it faced him, then glanced over each shoulder. 'You might want to back up a bit,' he suggested, licking his lips nervously as he fumbled in his pocket for the key.

I glanced at Tempest, but he nodded in an it's-best-to-play-along kind of way. So, obediently, I took a pace back and peered around the odd little man as he placed the key in the book's lock. When I spotted a bead of sweat on his brow, I couldn't help myself from asking, 'What's inside that book?'

He jumped at the sound of my voice in the quiet of the room and placed a hand on his heart. 'Goodness, I almost messed myself.' He gasped. Then he took a moment to compose himself and turned around so he could see everyone. 'The answer is that I don't know. I had to drive to Bedfordshire last night …'

'Bedfordshire?' echoed Tempest with a surprised look. 'That's got to be a hundred miles.'

'And a little more,' Frank replied. 'The book was there, and it represents the best chance of finding the information you want. I came straight here with it, which is why I haven't had a chance to see if the book is dangerous yet.'

Utterly perplexed, I stared wide-eyed at the book. 'How can a book be dangerous?'

Both Tempest and Big Ben groaned, making it clear I had asked the wrong question.

Frank's eyes sparkled though. 'This particular book is seven hundred years old and was written by the great wizard Falco Ironstorm. He fought many of the creatures written about within the covers of this tome and a sense of their power is almost certainly still trapped there. What we really need is a copper rod to connect it to Earth and some dragon's bane to protect ourselves from any immortal influences. Since we don't have any of those, I am wearing silver chain mail.' He pulled his shirt open a little to show us the glint of silver beneath. 'And I am wearing boots lined with fire lizard skin.'

I had to glance at Tempest again, but I got the same expression as last time; sort of yes-he's-nuts-but-you-can-trust-him all contained in a shrug.

Unable to think of anything else to say, I mumbled, 'Okay.'

Frank turned back to the book. Tilted his head left and right as if limbering up and then swooped, turning the key and jumping back as if trying to avoid getting stung or shocked. He had his arms out to either side to protect the rest of us as he cringed his face to one side, afraid of what might happen next.

Nothing happened.

I pursed my lips and stared.

No one said anything, and just when I thought we were all going to stay like that for the rest of the morning, Frank dropped his arms and visibly relaxed. 'Vermont must have diffused it before he turned it over to me. He would know to do that, of course.'

Tempest sounded surprised when he asked, 'You got this from Vermont Wensdale?'

'Who's Vermont Wensdale?' I asked, once again feeling like I was ill-informed or had come in halfway through a conversation.

'He's a famous monster hunter responsible for ridding this realm of many hundreds of seemingly unstoppable beasts,' Frank told me, then to Tempest, said, 'Yes. He's in Dunstable tracking a Nosferatus, a real mean one it is too.'

Now content the book was safe, Frank opened it. As we crowded around, the doorbell rang at the other end of the house.

'I'll get it,' rang out Barbie's voice. It sounded like she was near the front door so had probably changed from her sports outfit into a business suit and had been coming down the stairs.

With a muttering of annoyance at his blonde friend's insistence of messing with his butler duties, Jermaine started for the door. Barbie wouldn't actually open it, but she, like me, liked to tease him about the glacial pace he always moved in when in his butler role. He would never be hurried, always striding slowly and purposefully, his nose held aloft as he went about running the household. Barbie knew he would hurry to make sure she wasn't trying to open the door but would then appear in the entrance hallway moving at his usual slow pace.

As he left, the rest of us peered into the book. Frank had donned a pair of white gloves, to protect the ancient paper I assumed, but when I

74

reached forward to point at a drawing on a page, he slapped my hand away. 'That's not ink, Patricia, please do not touch it.'

Big Ben laughed. 'Let me guess; its werewolf blood?'

Frank sighed. 'Don't be silly, Ben. Everyone knows werewolf blood would fade and become invisible after a century or so. This is the bile from a ghoul.' He held up a hand to stop any further questions. 'If you are about to ask why they would use it, the answer is that it has great binding properties. The toxicity depletes the background magic of the words to limit the latent danger the book would otherwise present.'

I butted in, 'I think we should let Frank continue.' Please, before he spouts anymore ridiculous nonsense.

'Thank you, Patricia,' he replied. Then he turned a few more pages and arrived at a drawing of a creature that was part goat and part man. 'This is Quentiox,' he announced. Tracing along a line with one finger, he began reading the ancient text. It was written in old English. Or perhaps that should be olde English. Either way, I couldn't read it so had to watch Frank's lips move as he prepared to translate it. After a minute or so, he straightened and looked dead ahead into the distance. All he had to say was, 'Oh, dear.'

'What, oh dear?' asked Tempest. When he got no answer, he lifted an arm, stuck out a finger and prodded Frank in the arm.

Frank snapped out of his reverie. 'Sorry,' he mumbled.

Before I could find out what was troubling him, Jermaine reappeared from the front of the house carrying a large bouquet of flowers. In each hand. Then, Barbie came through the door behind him carrying two more. Finally, Molly walked in behind Barbie and she had two bouquets as well. Barbie was grinning at me, Jermaine bore his usual unreadable butler's expression, and Molly just looked nervous.

It was sufficient interruption to break the spell Frank had woven. 'What's this?' I asked.

'Flowers for you, madam,' replied Jermaine stating the obvious.

'From an admirer,' added Barbie with a mischievous wink.

'I've never seen so many flowers,' said Molly, staring agog at the two bunches she held. 'My boyfriend only ever gets me the crap ones from the petrol station when he wants to get in my knickers.' Big Ben burst out laughing, and Molly's face reddened as she realised what she had just said. She blurted, 'Begging your pardon, madam,' following it with a curtsy to hide her face.

'No curtsying, Molly,' I reminded her for the hundredth time. 'I am not royalty, and you can call me Patricia or Mrs Fisher if you prefer. I plucked a note in a tiny envelope from a stick poking out of the bouquet nearest me.

Barbie asked, 'Who's it from?' Her excitement bubbling over.

The note read:

Looking forward to getting to know you better,

David Sebastian

'It's from the lord mayor,' I murmured, surprised to receive flowers from anyone.

Barbie squealed. 'He's ever so handsome, Patty. Is it a saucy note or is he being a gentleman?'

I stuck the note back into the flowers. 'This is a distraction. We have a case to solve and too little time to be wasting it on nonsense like flowers. Please keep one bouquet, Jermaine, and have the rest given to the church or the ladies at the knitting circle; they meet today.'

He said, 'Very good, madam,' and about faced, taking the bouquets from Barbie and shooing Molly from the room as he left. I turned my attention back to Frank. 'Frank, you look troubled. What is written in the book?'

He bowed his head. 'It says that Quentiox is the giver of power. His true followers will each be bestowed with greatness and wealth as he inhabits them to smite their enemies and unshackle them from the efforts of those who might prevent their rise.'

'Okay, well that just sounds like the cult people have found themselves someone to worship. Why are they sacrificing people?'

He sighed as if carrying a great burden. 'Quentiox was rare as a pagan god. Most of the deities worshipped by the pagans were benign, drawing on Earth power to give to their followers. Quentiox was too thirsty for power and the other gods turned on him. He fought them and almost won but was entombed in the earth more than a thousand years ago. I suspect, though it doesn't say, that his demand for blood sacrifices was what enraged the other gods. Either way, he is recorded as being buried under the cusp of Orion and Orion will reach its solstice tomorrow. It is a celestial event that only happens once every two and a half thousand years.'

I mulled that over, Tempest asking a question before I could. 'The cult intends to raise Quentiox then? That is their intention. They will sacrifice a bunch of women because they think it will raise him. Then what? There's a giant immortal god stomping around destroying stuff?'

Frank shook his head. 'It's more subtle than that and far, far worse.'

'How so?' I gasped.

With a dread voice, Frank locked his eyes on mine. 'The high priest you described. He will channel the ancient god and become him. Whether he then dispenses his powers to his followers or just uses them for his own gain, I can only speculate, but Quentiox, if one reads the subtext of his actions, is inherently selfish. He is all about personal gain, preying on the greed of men to attract followers. It's probably why he was so popular. At the ceremony, the high priest will drink the blood of his sacrifices and transform from human to god as Quentiox inhabits his mortal form. After that, he will be unstoppable – they only stopped him before because the other gods had enough following to rival him when brought together. That was when pagan gods were *the* belief system. Now, their followers are so scattered that the gods have no power at all.' Frank began to weep, his shoulders shaking as emotion overcame him. 'I fear we are all doomed.'

Tempest put a hand on the smaller man's shoulder. 'Okay, Frank. Stiff upper lip there, old boy. We'll track them down and stop the ceremony.' He and I exchanged a look where we both rolled our eyes.

Between sobs, Frank managed, 'You can count me in, Tempest. Be sure of that. I shall open my arsenal and be ready for your call. We shall die side by side as we face down a god this time.'

A short while later, Tempest had calmed Frank down and helped him get all the books and things into his car. He was heading for his bookshop, where I imagined his assistant Poison was going to have an odd day attempting to console the strange little man. I commented that I found his volunteering to die so readily surprising, but Tempest assured me the man had the heart of a lion. Big Ben then added that Frank had balls the size of Bristol, but I pretended not to hear his comment.

We each of us had assigned tasks and it was time to get about them. Barbie and I were heading to Maidstone police station.

I let Barbie drive, or rather, I encouraged her to do so. The Maharaja had left a garage full of cars at my disposal. They were mine now, or so the paperwork said, but I still felt quite discombobulated about it all. The house I was getting used to, but the garage full of cars still felt too much.

My Aston Martin, the one car in the collection that was actually mine, was still on its way back and we were not going to wait for it. I made sure Anna was walked but then had to get going. I would have happily driven, but Barbie was unused to British roads, and kept ducking the chance to drive unless she could take the Mini Cooper.

'What if I scratch one?' she wailed when I said she should drive. Then she gasped, 'What if I crash one?'

'Then they are all insured,' I said as calmly as I could though I had to admit the idea of destroying one of the insanely expensive cars concerned me enough that I almost always took my own car. Staring at the selection, and biting her lip, as she tried to choose the one she might feel safest in, I knew she wanted to pick the Mini Cooper so had asked Jermaine to take it first. He was going to Canterbury and would rather have taken the Bentley. However, he agreed without comment and wished me luck with his blonde friend at the wheel. I knew it would help her to learn to drive on the English roads and give her the confidence to get out by herself more. Our roads are tight compared to California and never more so than in the countryside where she now lived. Many roads near us were only wide enough for one car, resulting in lots of backing up to find a passing place.

'How about the red one?' I prompted.

'The Ferrari?' she squeaked, terrified at the idea. 'That thing is worth more than a house.'

'But not this house,' I countered.

She continued to argue. 'They're your cars, Patty. You should drive.'

'They are the house's cars. Not mine. The gift from the Maharaja was for saving his crown and his country from the rule of his uncle. I seem to remember you being a big part of that. Now pick a car or I'll pick one for you,' I growled. She knew I was joking but gave in and picked a bunch of keys from the cabinet.

Only when she held them up did I realise she had snagged a set at random. 'Which car are these for?' she asked as the key fob swung around to reveal a raging bull.

Ten minutes later, she was over her fear and shrieking with delight as the Lamborghini powered through the countryside leaving a swirling maelstrom of autumn leaves in its wake.

At the police station, I dialled the number Mike gave us for Police Constable Patience Woods. She answered on the first ring, 'Hey, yo. Is that Patricia Fisher?'

'Yes, hello, Patience. Mike Atwell said you would be able to help us speak to Simon and Steven in the crime lab.'

'Only too happy to help out. Park along the road in the public car park and come to the front desk. I'll meet you there.'

So that was what we did, the short black woman smiling as she held a door open to take us into the station. Barbie's eyes were scanning around as she tried to take everything in. 'Wow, this place is nice. Patty and I ended up in some horrible police cells, didn't we Patty? The stations were always just as bad.'

Patience gave her a disbelieving look. 'Girl, you look like a Disney Princess and I mean like a cartoon one where their eyes are twice the size they should be, and their waists are so small a person has to wonder if they ever eat anything.' She snagged a box of donuts as she walked, and said, 'Talking about eating always makes me hungry. Donut, ladies?' she wafted the box under my nose, but I caught Barbie giving me side eye, and declined.

It was a good thing I did because they weren't hers. When the man who had left them unattended returned to his desk, he looked around, spotted her making a beeline for a door, and shouted, 'Those are mine, Woods!' Then he started chasing her.

Patience crammed one into her mouth, chewing as fast as she could and then snagged a second which turned out to be the last in the box. As she threw the empty container in a trash bin, she flipped the man the bird, barged the door open with her bum and vanished through it mumbling something around the crumbs. I think it was supposed to be, 'You snooze, you lose,' but I honestly couldn't tell.

The route through the station took too many left and right turns for me to know where I was or hope to find my way out again. However, we reached a door marked crime lab and Patience led us inside where Simon was bent over a scope of some kind, his eyes pressed to the eye pieces as he inspected something below.

Steven stood on the other side of the room with a bucket of something at his feet. I wasn't going to ask what it was, but they both looked up when Patience slammed the door. 'You have to get their attention,' she advised us both knowingly. 'I'll be by the door watching for Quinn. He won't like finding you two in here.'

'No, he wouldn't like that at all,' agreed Steven. 'He hates anything to disturb the crime lab and he brought us all manner of pointless scrapings and fibres from the thing out in Newington last night.'

I advanced toward Steven, my hand out for him to shake, but he held his own hand up to show me it was encased in a green glove which was in turn covered in a gloopy slime of some kind.

'You don't even want to know what this is,' he told me, backing away to a sink so he could wash up. Both men wore lab coats today as a change to the on-scene attire I had seen them in on previous encounters.

Simon switched off his scope and spun around on his seat. 'Mike said you have a dagger for us with some chemical residue on it?' His eyebrows were raised as he looked us both over. He couldn't see it because it was in my handbag; I doubted it was ever a good idea to walk into a police station with a knife and quite especially not when it is a vital piece of evidence one has pilfered from a crime scene. I placed it carefully into his hands still in the plastic bag Tempest put it in the previous night.

'Oh, yes,' said Simon. 'This would almost certainly be the weapon that was used to murder Gerard Gallagher.'

'Or one very much like it,' added Steven, his hands now clean.

Simon placed it carefully into a tray as four of us crowded around two sides of a stainless-steel bench. Carefully, Simon opened the bag so he could tip the contents out. Both men bent at the waist so they could get close enough to sniff it, their faces both masks of concentration as they closed their eyes to shut out other influences. They reminded me of Anna sniffing at interesting smells to determine what they were.

'CHP?' asked Simon.

'Possibly,' his partner replied, both straightening again. 'It has that sharp smell.'

'It narrows down which test to use, at least.'

'Yes,' replied Steven, the two scientists happily conducting their own conversation without involving the three women.

'CHP?' I asked, echoing Simon but this time asking what the heck it was.

As Simon carried the knife to a different machine and placed it inside, Steven explained. 'Concentrated Hydrogen Peroxide. It is a versatile product with many, many uses.'

I prompted more, 'Such as?'

'H_2O_2 is found in hair care products such as shampoos and hair dyes and in a lot of cleaning products. It's great for cleaning toilets and mouldy bathrooms. It appears in medical products as an antiseptic and occurs freely in our own bodies. Once concentrated, it can be used as a bleaching agent, an oxidizer or an antiseptic.'

Barbie put her hand up like she was in class. 'What is an oxidizer?'

'Good question,' Steve acknowledged. 'In chemistry, an oxidizing agent is a substance that has the ability to oxidize other substances — in other words to accept their electrons. Common oxidizing agents are oxygen, hydrogen peroxide and the halogens. Does that answer your question?'

'Oh, yeah,' snorted Patience from over by the door. 'It's all clear now.'

Behind Steven, the machine Simon was using beeped. He leaned in to read from its screen. 'It is hydrogen peroxide in a concentrated form.'

I waited for him to tell me more, but it was clear after a few seconds that he had exhausted his list of information. 'Why is it on the dagger? I asked.

'No time!' squealed Patience, 'Quinn is walking this way.'

Quickly, Simon said, 'That I cannot tell you. There were some other trace elements, but nothing substantial. I'll print you a read off.' He hit a button, the machine beeped, and piece of paper was thrust toward me. I put it and the dagger back into my pocket moments before the door opened.

'What are you doing in here, Woods?' demanded Chief Inspector Quinn.

'She was just showing us out,' I lied before anyone else could speak. 'I had a theory I wanted to share with the gentlemen here and they agreed to listen to me. It would seem, though, that I am barking up the wrong tree.'

CI Quinn gave me suspicious eyes. 'What theory?'

'That the kidnapped women are being held in a residence connected with one of the cult members. There were lots of expensive cars there last night. I hoped your crime lab chaps might be able to access satellite recordings of the vehicles leaving the scene, but apparently that kind of technology only exists on television.'

The chief inspector had to suppress a laugh at my ludicrous suggestion, which was the point of my lie. 'Yes, Mrs Fisher. I'm afraid we are not that technologically advanced yet. Give it another hundred or so years, though I expect by then people will be using teleporters and not cars. Woods escort these ladies back to reception.'

I nodded my thanks at Steven and Simon as Barbie and I made our way silently to the door. The chief inspector held out a hand to stop us leaving though. 'Mrs Fisher, I have to say that I do not endorse your private investigation business. I will however tolerate it, even support it on occasions if you are able to achieve results that bring criminals to justice. I cannot, however, allow you to access police resources, so I want to make it clear that I do not expect to find you in this lab again.'

'Thank you, Chief Inspector,' I replied, my voice neutral as I silently gloated over a victory he would never know of.

Patience was waiting for us, her eyes wide as she waited to see if her superior would have any more to say. He didn't, and we were free to leave but we only got a few feet before he changed his mind. 'Mrs Fisher, you have a client who believes his daughter is one of the alleged captives, is that correct?'

'Yes. Helena Gallagher. Since her husband was murdered thirty-six hours ago and Linda Cole said she spoke to a woman calling herself Helena Gallagher, I am quite content to believe the cult have her.'

He nodded his understanding, choosing to not argue my point. 'I believe you can reassure your client. I believe we are very close to identifying the key members of this cult and to finding out where they have their intended victims stashed. The chief constable has personally placed me at the helm of the force that will take them down after my team uncovered several important items of evidence last night.'

'What evidence?' I found myself forced to ask. We had scoured the area and found nothing. Admittedly we were swift about it, but still ... I struggled to believe we had missed vital clues.

I got a deadpan face in reply to my question. 'I'm afraid I cannot divulge that information or the source it came from, Mrs Fisher. I will, however, promise to have one of my officers contact you when we have Helena Gallagher.'

I pursed my lips. He said source of evidence, which meant someone had provided a tip, not that they had found anything at the scene. He wasn't going to share it with me, but I focused on what was important, which was the recovery of the missing women. If the police got them and I missed out, then so be it; it wasn't a time for ego.

Seeing no sense in fighting the man currently holding all the cards, I said, 'Thank you, Chief Inspector.' He opened and held a door for us, and we followed Patience around the twisting route to get back to reception. We thanked her and left the station.

Outside, Barbie asked. 'Do you think they will catch them? I mean, do you think they have the clues they need to track down who is behind it?'

Walking back to the car, I said, 'I hope so.' It was my honest answer. I couldn't tell where Chief Inspector Quinn was in his investigation, but he couldn't be doing any worse than me. Thankfully, Barbie and I weren't the only ones working this case, so I called the guys to see if they had made out better than the girls.

Low Point

'There has been no activity at all, madam,' said Jermaine. He was in Canterbury, sitting in the same cafeteria window Tempest and I had occupied yesterday. I thought the chances of Mortice Keys returning to his shop were thin. He must have seen Tempest and me at the ritual last night. Not that I had seen him. Despite his size, there had been other people wearing the simple white robe with similar figures. However, I felt confident he was there since I had seen his car when Tempest and I slunk between them.

'How long have you been there?'

'Less than an hour, madam.'

'Any sign of the police?'

'No, madam. However, my focus is on the shop front and the windows at the front of the property. The police could easily have another vantage point from which they are watching.'

'Okay. The chemical thing was a bust. It was something called concentrated hydrogen peroxide which is found in half the products on the planet by the sound of it. The man holding it before Tempest got it might have just washed his hair and left a trace of shampoo behind.' I was still irked that it led us nowhere and was trying to think my way clearly to the next step.

Jermaine said, 'I believe I should remain here a while longer unless you have another task for me, madam.'

'No. Stay there for now. Check in if anything happens.'

'Very good, madam.'

I had the phone on speaker in the car, so Barbie heard the whole thing. 'What about Tempest and Big Ben?' she asked as she manoeuvred through traffic funnelling out of Maidstone.

I nodded as I pressed the button to connect me to Tempest's phone. It went to voicemail, so I left a quick message to tell him we were heading back to my house and that the visit to the station gained us nothing.

No sooner had I recorded it, than he called me back. 'Patricia. I couldn't answer your call until I moved position. We found Anthony Perkins, but he was ... evasive?'

'Evasive?'

'Yes. I expected to find him at work, but the staff said his car had been stolen last night and he was staying at home to deal with it. I sent Big Ben just in case he recognised me from last night. I stayed around the corner but listened to their brief conversation.'

'How brief was it?'

'Big Ben pretended to be a detective assigned to investigate the theft of his car, but he called him out straight away because two uniformed officers had visited less than an hour before we got there. Dropping the pretence, Big Ben asked him where he had the women stashed. And then wanted to know what would happen to the ceremony tomorrow night if Anthony didn't make it because he was in hospital having both feet removed from his rectum.'

'Oh, Lord! What did he do then?'

'Anthony Perkins tried to slam the door in Big Ben's face. It's not a tactic that works. It just bounced off his foot. Anthony threatened to call the police and Big Ben encouraged him to do so. Neither of us believed his story about the car being stolen and Big Ben knows facial cues well enough to read when a person is lying. I left my hiding spot at that point which is how I got to see the mark on his face.'

'Go on,' I encouraged, keen to hear what he was trying to tell me. 'When I went for Linda last night, I disarmed the man with the knife first and I did it with an elbow to his right cheekbone. Anthony Perkins has a nasty bruise to his right cheek and if I was a betting man, I would say it was less than twenty-four hours old. Not only was he there, he was one of the ones who brought Linda out when she was to be sacrificed. He might know where the women are being held.'

Feeling an urgent need to know more, I asked, 'So what happened next?'

'He knew we weren't police and weren't going to arrest him, and I honestly had to toss up whether to beat the truth out of him or leave in the hope that he might go out later and lead us to them.'

'I thought his car was gone?' queried Barbie.

'There were still four to choose from on his driveway. Anyway, we pulled back and monitored the house but then I got to thinking about the chemicals on the dagger and I am currently at his business waiting for the guys in the warehouse to go for lunch. I want to have a look around and see if there is anything untoward going on.'

I grimaced. 'I wouldn't bother, Tempest. We just left the crime lab. The chemical is just an ordinary every day compound found in shampoo and other household products.'

Tempest said a bad word and then apologised. 'This is a whole lot of dead ends, isn't it?'

I blew out a breath. 'It sure is. I feel like we have hit a low point. Nothing is getting us any closer to finding the victims.'

'Is it worth telling Chief Inspector Quinn about Anthony Perkins?' suggested Barbie.

We heard a harrumph from Tempest. 'I already did. He wasn't interested. He said the car was reported stolen and would be investigated as a separate crime, and that admitting assault would not work in my favour. Truth be told, he might be working the Perkins angle and just pretending he isn't because that's the sort of thing he does. He never tells anyone what he is doing just in case it doesn't work; easier to deny that way.'

I gritted my teeth and tried to rally, but I was failing. I just couldn't see the next logical step to take. Everywhere we looked, we hit another dead end. I couldn't be defeated like that though. 'Tempest I'm heading for home. There must be something I have missed, something that ties people together. We only have two cult members identified so far but maybe there is something in their past that links them.'

'Yes. I am not of a mind to give up yet. I think I will poke around this warehouse anyway. It's 1157hrs so I'll hang on for their lunch break and if Mr Perkins makes a move, Big Ben and I will tail him.'

We wished each other better luck than we'd been having and ended the call.

Barbie asked, 'Have you noticed he always uses a twenty-four-hour clock when he tells the time?'

A little snort of laughter escaped my nose. 'He's ex-military. Not that I think all former soldiers are like that, but I'm sure that's where he gets it from.'

We travelled the rest of the journey in silence, Barbie trying not to enjoy the car too much and me trying to work out why I couldn't find a corner to pick at – this was an elusive case and I wasn't used to having such a ticking clock; I could almost hear it ticking. More often, I investigated murder and the victim was already dead; I could take my time if I chose to and often mixed one investigation up with others. Now, I felt sleep wasn't even an option.

As we came back through West Malling High Street, my phone rang. The number came up as unknown, which generally meant it was being withheld by the caller. It could be telesales or some other nonsense, but I was curious enough to answer.

'Patricia Fisher.'

'Hold please.'

That was all I got. A woman's voice asking me to hold. It might have been polite, but I chose to hang up anyway. It was only that the request caught me by surprise that delayed me stabbing the end call button by long enough for a new voice to come on the line.

'Patricia, good day to you. This is David Sebastian. Did you get my flowers?'

Barbie grinned at me. I ignored her, and very much ignored the increased heartrate I got without asking for. 'Yes, thank you, David. One bouquet would have done it. To what do I owe this call?'

'I was rather hoping I might entice you out for afternoon tea. Are you available today? I can clear my diary if you are.'

Barbie mouthed the word, 'Score!' and pumped her fist in the air. I was quite happy being single thank you very much.

'I'm afraid I won't have time, David. I cannot clear my diary for any social engagements any time soon.'

'I understand,' he replied brightly. 'You have a business to run and crooks to catch. Do you have a big case currently?'

Creasing my brow, I voiced my confusion, 'You know I do, David. You saw me pursuing it last night.'

'Oh,' he sounded genuinely surprised. 'I thought the chief constable ordered you to drop it.'

'Ordered me?' my response came out a little more snappy than I intended it to. 'How would he do that? At best he could make a polite request. I have a client and legal right to investigate.'

'Yes. Yes, of course,' the lord mayor quickly backpedalled. 'I just meant that I assumed you would move on to a less controversial case.'

'And I will do so just as soon as I have solved this one.' I cut over the top of him, wanting to wrap the conversation up since Barbie had just pulled into the driveway to our property and we would be at the house in seconds.

Sensing my desire to end the call, David bowed out gracefully. 'I can see that I have caught you at a bad time, Patricia. I hope that we can be friends. If you change your mind about joining me for dinner at any point, please let me know. I'll have my personal assistant provide you with contact details. Speak soon I hope.'

The line went dead and I felt like a heel. By the end of our call, he managed to sound like a puppy I had chosen to kick.

'You're really not interested in him?' asked Barbie, swinging the car around to the garage at the back of the house.

I wasn't sure how to answer. He was handsome and trim, he was warm and engaging. Maybe it was simply too soon after my last romantic affair. Maybe it was something else, but as I gave Barbie a shrug so I could avoid answering, I had to ask myself if there was something about him that I just didn't trust.

Research

I had Anna snuggled on my lap as Barbie and I tucked into some lunch – a healthy one because I was with Barbie. She is impossible to argue with because I know she is right when she argues nutrition.

Next to Anna was Georgie, the one girl from the litter. After a tough morning of doing almost nothing, they were now exhausted and needed to sleep it seemed. Barbie had three tiny boy puppies arranged on a cushion on her lap as she scrolled, clicked, and ransacked the internet. They were sleeping too, the three of them all in a line with their noses beneath her left elbow and their tails all in a line over her right thigh.

'What about Anthony Perkins?' asked Barbie, pulling up a social media profile for him. She had checked him a bit last night, but it was late then, and we were all tired. There wasn't a lot to learn from the popular sites; he wasn't a person who bothered to post about his life to others. She switched to looking at his company and his wider family, pulling up a separate search for Mortice Keys using his real name, Arthur Poole, at the same time to see if we could find a connection somewhere. Both men had multiple children, four for Mortice and three for Anthony, all adults now which extended the search because the connection might be through their children's' university attendance or work or joint membership at a club. I was scribbling physical notes and drawing lines between ideas, but we were fast approaching the point where would have to admit we had gone down a rabbit hole.

Barbie pointed to the screen. 'Here's something.' I looked up from my notepad. 'Ten months ago, the biggest rival to Telelift, Anthony Perkins' firm, was burned to the ground in a fire that was suspected arson.' I looked at the photographs of a fire raging at night as firefighters did their best to quell the blaze. 'I found it by accident because I was looking at his books and found a massive spike. His business has been going twenty years and doing steadily until two years ago when its profit and turnover started to rise. Then it skyrocketed as we came into this year. It could be nothing ...' she admitted.

'Or it could be something. Have you looked at Mortice Keys' books yet?'

'I was just about to.'

We studied them together, both jumping when we saw a similar spike occurring eighteen months ago. It drove Barbie to search for events which might have caused it. Finally feeling that we might be onto something, I opened a second laptop which I used to continue looking for a connection. Thirty minutes of silence followed as Barbie and I both stared at our screens as we looked for the answers. None came.

When my phone rang, Anna popped her head up to grump me because I leaned too far and woke her up; dachshunds are so intolerant. The caller was Jermaine.

Buoyed by hope, I answered, 'Jermaine?'

'Good afternoon, madam. There is movement inside the shop. It started just a few moments ago but the lights are not on.' No lights on meant the person or people inside were trying to remain unseen or disguise what they were doing. They didn't want anyone to see and that had to mean they were up to no good.

I made a split-second decision. 'Stay there, I'm coming to you.'

'Very good, madam.'

I jumped out of my chair, snagging Anna under one arm; she was coming with me since I felt I had left her at home too often recently. Barbie got a hand of support on her shoulder and a kiss to the top of her head. 'Good luck, Barbie. Let me know if you find the link or anything else worth reporting. I'm going to follow a hunch and see where it leads.'

She grabbed my arm as I turned to leave. 'I think I may have already found it.' She was reading the screen at speed, her eyes dancing across the words which made my foot twitch. I wanted to go right now, but if she had something pertinent … 'They went to the same school,' her voice came out as a whisper almost. Then she nodded to herself. 'Yes. I'm not wrong. Both men were in the same class as children. They joined Hartford Boys' Academy at eleven; what would that be? Seventh Grade?'

Looking over her shoulder at the information displayed, I said, 'That would depend on whether one counts a reception year or not. I think you call it Kindergarten, but children in the UK transition to senior school at eleven so that makes sense.' I felt a surge of adrenalin. 'Who else was in their class?'

Barbie blew out a breath to calm herself. 'Leave it with me. You go help the butler. I'll see if I can't find a school photograph and a list of children who attended.'

Now that she was finding things, I kind of wanted to stay but I knew I wouldn't add much value, so I was better employed elsewhere. Then, just as I was leaving, a thought occurred to me. 'What school did David Sebastian go to?'

Barbie's head snapped around. 'Really? He's the lord mayor. Surely, you can't think he's involved? You are an attractive woman of a not too dissimilar age, Patty. He could just want to date you. I think that more likely than he is targeting you as part of his master plan.'

The inside of my skull was itching. 'Can you look it up anyway?'

She sighed but clicked the mouse to open a new search. I knew Jermaine was waiting but I couldn't shift the feeling that I had just stumbled onto something. Thirty seconds and a few clicks later, Barbie jabbed a finger at the screen. 'I'm sorry, Patty. He just likes you.' Anthony Sebastian went to Tonbridge Secondary. It was there for anyone to see on his personal biography and mirrored in his social media profile.

Accepting that my senses were off, I snatched up my handbag and hurried to the door. Over my shoulder, I called. 'Let me know if you find anything.'

I was heading for Canterbury, a quick shot down the motorway at this time of the day. Jermaine might have something worth investigating, but as I slid into my vintage silver Aston Martin, I had to admit to myself that I was surprised how far off the mark my intuition was today.

Later, I would find out just how blind my senses were.

On the way to Canterbury I called Tempest to tell him what we had discovered.

'That's a great link to find. I'll get Jane on it too. She can liaise with Barbie and see what they turn up together; two heads and all that. Neither of those men could be the high priest though; they are both the wrong shape or height. He's still unidentified as are all the followers in the crowd. Two people isn't enough, and the link is only tenuous.'

'Yes, Barbie is trying to get hold of a roster from the school for that class.' I wondered if I should mention the lord mayor and decided it couldn't hurt. 'What's your impression of the lord mayor?'

'The guy from last night. He sent you the flowers, right, but you're not asking me for relationship advice, are you? You suspect he could be involved?'

'No. Maybe.' I realised how indecisive I sounded. There was something in what Tempest had just said about the size of the high priest – he was the same size as the lord mayor. I chose to not embarrass myself by mentioning it. 'I guess I haven't decided yet. He seems very eager. Barbie thinks he is just being romantic and forward, but I get an itch at the back of my skull when I think about him and that usually means I am onto something. He didn't go to their school though and grew up in a totally different area so if the school connection isn't a red herring, then he looks unlikely to fit the frame.'

'Plus, politicians have to be squeaky clean these days,' Tempest added.

I sighed. It was beginning to look more and more like I had attracted a new romantic interest and I really didn't know how to feel about that. Alistair, the captain of the Aurelia was thousands of miles away, probably

99

on the other side of the world and we made no commitment to each other even if he had left it open for me to return.

'How did you get on at the warehouse?' I asked to change the subject.

'It was ... odd,' he replied, stuttering a little as if trying to find the right word. 'The warehouse is full of parts and assemblies for the stair lifts and things the firm makes but there was a door leading to another area. On the door was a sign telling the staff it was private and they were not allowed to go in. It struck me as very strange – what could possibly be in there? I almost got caught, in fact. I had to go out the back window, but I picked the lock and went inside, and they have a full chemical cooking plant set up inside.'

'What are you saying?' I asked, unsure what I was supposed to understand from his comment.

'It looked like I might imagine a crystal meth plant might look. By which I mean it was a little messy and had a ton of chemistry equipment in there and was hidden away where no one would see it.'

'Did you find drugs?'

'No, not a thing. Whatever they had been cooking down had been shipped already. It's a great site for it though. The unit is right at the edge of an industrial estate, there are no houses around so a person working at night wouldn't be seen and the same would be true for vehicles coming and going during hours when the business is closed so that staff there might never know.'

I nodded along as he talked, wondering if maybe we had this all wrong from the start and the pagans/cult/whatever you want to call them were all about drugs instead. 'Why the sacrifices then?' I asked. 'If they are drug dealers or manufacturers or whatever, why are they kidnapping people and killing them to prove fealty to a pagan god?'

'That is a question I would love an answer to, but I could be way off the mark with the drugs thing. They could be using the chemistry set for something else entirely, something to do with the products they manufacture, and the staff are banned from going in because they are not qualified. It could just be a health and safety thing.'

I ran that through my head. 'I don't buy it.'

'Me neither,' Tempest agreed. 'Until we know more, there is no point alerting the police and I don't have enough credit to get a friendly police officer to look into it.' My thoughts flashed to Mike Atwell. Yesterday, he could have got a sniffer dog in there with one click of his fingers. Not now though, I suspected. Tempest broke my train of thought. 'I'm going back to relieve Big Ben. He'll need to get some lunch, but I haven't heard from him so it's safe to assume Mr Perkins hasn't left the house yet. We'll stay on him until something else comes up, but I'll call Jane and get her looking at possible connections the two men might have to other prominent figures in the area.'

By the time the call ended, I was less than ten minutes out from Canterbury, the rest of the trip flashing by as I worked the problem around and around in my head. Next to me, on the passenger seat, Anna slept, waking only when I pulled off the motorway to cruise into the city.

I drove by the shop, checking to see if Jermaine was still in the café and then parked in a space along the road. With Anna pulling at her lead and excited to be somewhere new, I walked back toward Mortice Keys' shop, Earth Magic, Jermaine appearing in the street before I reached the café.

'Madam,' Jermaine greeted me.

'Is it him?' I asked getting straight to the point.

'I have not been able to ascertain that, but they were still in there just a few minutes ago. I took a walk around to the back of the shop, but Mr Keys' car is not there.' It meant it probably wasn't him; Mortice Keys did not appear to be a person who walked much.

I was here now, so I shrugged and said, 'Okay, let's go have a look.'

Crossing the road, unless a person were to recognise me, I looked like a woman walking her dachshund. Jermaine, walking at my side could be my friend, a partner, or anything. The point is, having a dog is always a great disguise. On this occasion, it made no difference because as we sidled casually up to the door as if we were customers expecting the shop to be open, the two men inside froze, exchanged a glance, and bolted.

I said a very unladylike word in my surprise but then slapped Jermaine on his arm as I yelled, 'Break it!'

I got a, 'Yes, madam,' in response and though he said it calmly, his whole body was already moving. Rotating off his left foot, his right leg came up and out, striking the door just below the handle as it was only half extended. His foot didn't stop or bounce off though, it drove straight through, exploding the lock and splintering the door. The top and bottom security bolts kept it in place, but it was folded about its centre so when he kicked it again, the top half let go and swung inward at an angle. Then he took off running down the street, his voice echoing back, 'I'll cut them off at the rear, madam.'

There was nothing for it. I had to go in and make sure they couldn't escape this way because there were two exits and only one ninja butler. I needed a weapon – something blunt, I didn't want to kill anyone, but as I looked around, I heard urgent footsteps coming my way.

Unwelcome fear gripped me, I wasn't a fighter by any means, but I knew catching the men I saw inside the shop might be the difference between saving the missing women and not. Jermaine might be chasing them toward me, but I was the one who had to stop them, so as fear made my legs feel weak, I put Anna on the floor and looked around. That was when I noticed the shop had been ransacked. It looked to have been burgled. The display cabinet which yesterday had all manner of arcane items in it, was now almost empty and many of the items left were spilled onto the floor. I knew what they had taken, it was a ceremonial knife, but that hadn't been all they took; there was too much missing. Shelves had gaps where something had recently been removed and books were strewn across the floor as if the men had been looking for something they couldn't find.

I picked up a wooden candlestick. It was the kind designed to hold a church candle and was more than three feet tall. The price tag on it said it retailed for two hundred pounds and I almost put it down again to look for something cheaper to wield. I had no time to do so because a young man in a suit barrelled through the door that led from the back of the building into the shop. He had a sack over one shoulder which had to contain their stolen loot and he was quickly followed by another as I hefted the candlestick and swung it upward at his face.

Anna chose that moment to lunge at his feet, snarling viciously like she was going to tear his foot off. He yelped and jumped away from the terrifying beast, which meant my swing sailed through thin air. My target darted under my arms and out of the shop just as Anna snapped at his trouser leg. She got a tooth into it but was shaken free as he ran. The second man tried to jump her as she spun around to get him instead, but I had been able to correct my swing by then and managed to clout him over his shoulder and across the back of his neck.

He yelped in pain, but it was too little too late as he too sprinted through the ruined door of the shop and out into the street where he tore after his colleague. Anna went after him, running for all she was worth on tiny legs. Her breasts, saggy from feeding, flapped around as she nipped at the back-man's heels and she ignored my banshee screams as if deaf. Jermaine caught up to me, a little out of breath from the exertion. He intended to sprint after them, but I held him in place as a police car appeared a hundred yards away in a four-wheel drift as it skidded around the corner. Someone had seen us break in and called them.

A quick glance across the street revealed a dozen faces peering at us from inside the café.

This was bad. Really bad. Yesterday I was in there casing the joint.

'We have to get out of here! Right now!' I grabbed Jermaine's hand, whistled again for Anna and pulled him back into the shop. 'If they catch us in here, they will arrest us, and it will be morning before we get released. That's if Mortice Keys doesn't reappear and choose to press charges.'

Jermaine didn't argue. The police had listened to my claim that Mortice Keys had been at the ritual last night but that didn't mean they were doing anything about it, and if they were, it didn't mean they would find him. We had to get clear and circle around to get our cars when it was safe. I also needed to get my dog, but as I worried about her, I heard her paws scramble across the floor behind me. Jermaine and I had just made it through to the back part of the shop, but I went back for her and that was when I saw it.

She had stopped to sniff something on the carpet, her nose extended, and one paw lifted as she often did when being curious. Under her nose was a wallet.

'Madam, speed is of the essence,' Jermaine reminded me. I snagged the wallet and Anna and then I ran for all I was worth.

The Big Clue

The back of the shop led to an enclosed courtyard. It was how Jermaine had been able to cut them off and herd them back toward me. Now it meant we were about to be trapped ourselves. We both heard the cop car skid to a stop outside the shop followed by shouting as one gave instruction to the other. I had no doubt one was racing through the shop behind us and the other was sprinting around the corner to get to the courtyard.

We were going to get caught and that would leave the team to do the work short-handed. Exasperated by my luck, I straightened myself and checked my clothing. I would get arrested, but I would be dignified about it.

I didn't get the chance.

Before I could tell what was happening, an arm went under my bottom and lifted me high into the air. 'Hold onto Anna tightly, madam,' came Jermaine's advice as he ran across the courtyard. I wanted to demand that he put me down, but he clearly had a plan.

Shouts from the two cops, both male, echoed behind me, though when I tried to look, I could see neither. Jermaine ran behind a truck which obscured the view behind, hiding us from them. Then I went higher in the air as he climbed something.

'I'm going to lower you down, madam,' he whispered, as he changed his grip to hold me to his front. He had a massive hand on my hips, one each side and my face was to his for a moment as he lowered me over a fence. Had he dropped me, I would have survived, but noise from the fall would have attracted the officers who I could now hear accusing each other of missing us.

My feet hit the concrete and Jermaine let go. Then a shadow above made me look up just as he sailed over my head, performing a perfect somersault to land on his feet. Anna was struggling against me, not liking her trip through the air one little bit, but my hand over her mouth stopped her from barking. I needed her to stay quiet for just a few more seconds.

Jermaine crooked his arm for me to loop mine through and then we promenaded out of the yard on the other side of the fence as if we were walking along Brighton pier.

Through a small piece of serendipity, we were parked not far from each other, the Mini Cooper on the other side of the road and facing the other way, but we could escape the area without being seen as all the attention was on the front of the shop, not the two people getting into cars a hundred yards away. Jermaine spun his around and we set off on a circuitous route that would get us back to the motorway without taking us past the crowd and the police.

In my haste to capitalise on our escape, I didn't have time to check the wallet and now I was driving and risking not only my life but others if I attempted to do it now. Jermaine was in front of me as we cruised up the motorway, once again heading for the general vicinity of the Medway Towns and home. I flashed my headlights at him as we neared a service station and put my indicator on until he got the message and did the same.

I parked my car next to his. Giving Anna a pat as she raised her head, I reached across her for my handbag where the wallet had been speedily stashed. Inside, I found the usual paraphernalia of credit cards, debit cards and gym membership cards, several crisp twenty pound notes - which would go into the next charity box I saw - but what I wanted was the man's name and I had it.

107

I had no idea who James Whitmore was, but I knew a lady who could probably find out. The passenger door to my car opened as Jermaine joined me.

'How are you, madam?' he asked.

I shot him a mischievous grin and waggled my eyebrows. 'I'm great. I think we are closing the net. I just need to find out who this fellow is.' I showed him the driver's licence.

Jermaine said, 'Sterling work, madam,' as he scrutinised the contents of the wallet for any further information that might be pertinent – like a cult membership card, that would be handy. Especially if it came with a phone number and an address.

Barbie answered her phone straight away, the sound of her fingers on the keyboard sufficient to tell me she was still at the computer where I wanted her. 'Hey, Patty. Was the trip to Canterbury worth the effort?'

'You'll have to be the one to tell me that. Jermaine and I disturbed two men inside the shop. They escaped but one dropped his wallet. Can you look up the name James Whitmore, please?'

'James Whitmore?' she repeated, her voice blurting the words as if she had been shocked. 'I don't need to look it up, I've just been looking at him. He works with David Sebastian.'

'Oh, my God! I was right! The lord mayor was involved!' a wave of relief washed over me. 'Wait, why were you looking up David Sebastian?'

'Um,' she hesitated, which I knew was because she had been up to no good and was trying to think of something to say that would excuse what she was doing.

'You were trying to set me up with him, weren't you?' I accused her, my eyes narrowing at her even though she couldn't see them.

'Only sort of,' she whined. Then to distract me, she said. 'I've got all kinds of information about James here if you want it. He's twenty-eight, he has a law degree from Cambridge and a master's in economics from Oxford. He is the lord mayor's chief political strategist and worked with him for the last two years as they ran his campaign to gain office.'

What was he doing in Mortice Key's shop, that's what I wanted to know. Fortunately, I knew just the person to ask. 'Barbie, can you give me an address for David Sebastian's office? Where does the lord mayor reside when he is in his chambers?'

The lord mayor both resides in and operates from Canterbury, which makes sense as it is the county's capital city, has a famous cathedral, great road links to everywhere and sits almost central to everywhere else.

There was a nervous voice in my head telling me the police must have seen my car leaving the scene and were already searching for it. With that in mind, and because it stuck out so much, Jermaine and I took the Mini instead. It's a nice car but there are thousands of them around. His car also had satnav which made finding the place we wanted a lot easier.

We approached the building calmly and as if we belonged, rather than how I felt which was like a wanted woman who had just fled the scene of a crime.

Despite being a new role only invented this year, the lord mayor's office occupied a building that had to be at least five hundred years old. I suspected its original use was something to do with the church; there was religious symbology everywhere I looked and much of it carved into the stone.

Inside though, it had been fitted out with plush flooring and furnishings; a wide stainless-steel reception desk hiding just one small woman. I could only see her shoulders and head, but she had a flash of freckles across her nose and cheeks and green eyes beneath startling natural orange hair cut into a long bob that framed her round face perfectly. She looked up as we came in, flashing us a smile full of professional courtesy and white teeth. 'Good afternoon. Can I help you?'

'Hello, I'm Patricia Fisher,' I told her, guessing correctly that this was the lady who phoned me this morning just after the flowers were delivered. I saw the recognition in her eyes, so I played along. 'David sent me rather a lot of flowers this morning and I was hoping I might surprise him by dropping by.'

I got the impression the young woman wanted to say something about the situation but was professional enough to resist doing so. Instead, she gave me a crestfallen look. 'I'm sorry, David left early today. He has a big event tonight.'

I'll say he does! He's planning to murder a bunch of women!

I didn't say the words that presented themselves. I asked, 'Has he gone home? Perhaps I can catch up with him there.'

Again, she offered her disappointed face. 'No, he said he was going directly to the event to prepare.'

'What is the event please? Perhaps I can intercept him there.' I didn't for one minute think there was an event. He was going to the ritual tonight. I just didn't know what part he played in it.

The young woman glanced left and right, checking unnecessarily to see if we were being watched or overheard when there was no one else in the room. Satisfied that she could divulge the secret she held, she leaned forward to whisper, 'It's Ivor Biggun's birthday bash.'

I couldn't stop my eyebrows from rising. 'That's the internet sex chap, isn't it?' I asked.

She nodded. 'There are a lot of people going, but I was really surprised when David accepted the invitation because he spoke out about the degradation of society and erosion of morality in many of his speeches and railed about how pornography would destroy relationships for our children. He even launched a campaign to have Ivor Biggun's sites shut down. I think the invite came as a joke or a backhanded insult, but he's going tonight regardless.'

I tapped my right foot a little as I thought. Jermaine stood facing me, implacably calm yet poised should I have need for him to do anything. What should my next move be? The ritual had to be tonight. If the date for it was determined by celestial movements and the crazy people following those movements believed in all this nonsense, then they couldn't deviate. Was David Sebastian involved or not? I thanked the young woman and headed back out to the car with my tall butler escorting me. I talked it over with him.

'Jermaine, what do you think?'

'Madam?'

'Your gut reaction on the lord mayor. Do you think he might be the pagan high priest?'

'I couldn't possibly say, madam. He seemed pleasant and genuine, but that could be an act.'

He was right. It could be an act. The point, really, was that I couldn't prove it either way yet and though I knew a man who worked for him was taking things from Mortice Keys' shop, that in itself, was far from enough to convict the man. I remembered something else, the memory popping into my head unexpectedly. I gasped. 'The lord mayor had hat hair!'

'Madam?'

'Last night, when he was heading back to the helicopter, I saw a line going around the back of his head. The sort of mark one gets from wearing a hat.' Jermaine was waiting for me to explain. 'Or a ram's skull,' I filled in the blank.

'Or just a hat, madam. The lord mayor must have official robes to wear for his duties. Is it not likely that he has hats among his outfits?'

Dammit. Jermaine always made such a good sounding board for my ideas. I dismissed yet another clue I briefly thought might lead me somewhere.

Then my phone rang, my screen displaying a number I didn't recognise. 'Patricia Fisher, good afternoon.'

'Mrs Fisher, this is Chief Inspector Quinn, where are you please?'

I almost told him, but an uncomfortable feeling held me back. 'Why do you ask?'

'I have just reviewed footage from a CCTV camera in Edgbaston Road, Canterbury. It shows you and your butler, Jermaine Clarke, smashing your way into a shop. I have issued a warrant for your arrest. Please go to your nearest police station and surrender yourself.'

I thought for a moment. Telling him no would just result in him sending police to my house or anywhere else they might wish to look for me. So I said, 'Of course, Chief Inspector. It's all quite explainable. I'll go directly there.'

'Please make sure that you do, Mrs Fisher.' Then he ended the call. I couldn't tell if he believed me and frankly, I didn't much care. It did mean that I would have to step lightly now and keep out of sight as I tried to finish this case. I figured I had a little time, so Jermaine and I went back to collect my car and the two of us went home.

We congregated in the office at my house, Tempest leaving Big Ben to continue the stakeout at Anthony Perkins' house. That was beginning to look like yet another dead end and a potential waste of resources. We knew he was involved and that the police were not bothering to pursue him but if he stayed in the house and missed the ceremony then so would we.

Tempest said, 'I think we have to go to the party.'

I sucked air in between my teeth. Everyone was waiting to hear my opinion, but I made them wait several seconds while I ran it through my head again. I suspected David Sebastian of being involved in the pagan cult, maybe even of holding a high position in it, but all I had was a suspicion. The only tangible link was a member of his staff taking items from Mortice Keys shop. He hadn't broken in, so must have a key. I felt sure he was there to replace the ceremonial knife Tempest took; they would need it for the next ritual. Did that mean David had sent him?

Barbie prompted me. 'We have to consider that the party could be the venue for the ritual and that's why he is going there.'

'I agree,' I replied. 'However, I cannot help but feel that I am still clutching at straws; we don't have anything concrete yet. In fact, what I have isn't even circumstantial; it's just a gut feeling. So far, we have his chief strategist breaking into a shop which I can't report because then the police would know it was me there.'

'If they don't already,' added Barbie helpfully.

I grimaced at Jermaine. 'Yes. If they don't already.' The doorbell rang and Jermaine departed to answer it.

'If the ritual is at the party, it will take more than us to stop them and rescue the women. We would need the police, but I don't think I can sway Chief Inspector Quinn without hard evidence.'

'You won't,' Mike Atwell agreed as he strode into the room followed by Jermaine. 'He'll be playing ball with the chief constable now. I spoke to a couple of the guys at the station – actually they called me, but they said Quinn had an anonymous tip off from a person who claimed they used to be a cult member. Quinn knows where the ritual is being held and has a huge force primed to raid it as soon as he can confirm the missing women are there.'

Relief washed through me. This was the best news I could receive. Sure, it wouldn't be me that solved the case, but Helena Gallagher would be saved and that was good enough. The doorbell rang again; we were popular today.

'What about the lord mayor?' asked Tempest. If he is involved but isn't at the ritual, he will wriggle off the hook.' It was a good point, but it took me back to the part where I had to admit I had no good reason to suspect him other than a tenuous link to James Whitmore who might have been operating independently.

I talked it through with the team. 'Tempest, earlier you said, "Politicians have to be squeaky clean now because they live such public lives." If he were running around acting the role of high priest and running a cult that seeks to raise a pagan god, people would notice.'

'We don't know that he is the high priest, Patty,' Barbie pointed out. 'He could be just a member of the cult. An influential member maybe, but not necessarily the leader.'

I shook my head; that didn't feel right. 'I don't think he would settle for a minor role. Having met him, he comes across as the man who always leads. Besides,' I shrugged, 'there's nothing to link David Sebastian to either Mortice Keys or Anthony Perkins.'

'Actually, there is.' I looked up to see the small blonde woman from Tempest's office, the one who he told me was actually a guy. I tried to remember her name. Whether a man or a woman underneath, he or she looked every bit like a woman on the outside. A mop of blond hair swept over one shoulder which exposed a delicate neck on the other side. She wore a thin, knee-length cotton dress in a caramel colour and knee-high boots in a matching tone beneath. She looked thoroughly autumnal. Even her cross-body Radley messenger bag matched. She was narrow at the hips and chest but even believing it was a man underneath, I knew I would be shocked to discover it was.

She held up her hand to wave at the gathering. 'Hi, I'm Jane.'

'What have you for us, Jane?' asked Tempest.

She held a laptop in her left hand tucked against the side of her body. Barbie saw her looking around and made some space at the table for her. Opening it, Jane said, 'Tempest asked me to look into your case as deeply as I could and to see if I could find a link between David Sebastian and two other men who both went to the same school. It turns out they all went to the same school.'

Barbie's brow furrowed and she clicked the tab on her computer to bring up the information she had. 'He went to Tonbridge Secondary,' she argued, shaking her head. 'And he's not listed in the roster for the children in their year at Hartford Boys' Academy.'

'No, that's right,' Jane agreed, further confusing me and Barbie and probably everyone else. 'I found it by accident when I was looking at his father. David Sebastian's father was a professor of economics. He moved to a role at Hartford University when David was seventeen.' My eyes

116

widened as I saw the connection. Jane pointed to her screen where a graduation photograph showed three rows of young men in their school blazers. Right in the middle of the front row was David Sebastian. 'He moved to Hartford Boys' Academy in the final year for a single term. He was only there for four months.'

It was like a shaft of light shining down from heaven to illuminate the room. There was the connection. It was just too much coincidence to ignore. In a hushed tone, I said, 'He met them at school. How many others from that class are involved?'

'It could be all of them,' Mike answered. 'We cannot ignore the possibility that he is orchestrating the whole thing. Like Patricia said; he isn't the kind of man to take a back seat. I'd better call the chief inspector.'

Tempest tapped Jane on the arm. 'Why did you come here and not just call.'

She shrugged, her cheeks colouring slightly beneath her makeup. 'Dramatic effect.'

He chuckled at her but in a congratulatory way. 'Can you hack into the party and get us on the invite list? I think we should plan to go just in case the police don't believe us.'

In the corner, Mike was already arguing and going red in the face. His phone conversation sounded very one sided, but it was clear which way it was going. It ended abruptly a few seconds later with Mike offering to shove his job somewhere that I felt quite sure the chief inspector wouldn't want it. Then he mimed strangling his phone with both hands before sensing that we were all watching him.

Tempest asked, 'We're on our own, right?'

With an apologetic sigh, Mike said, 'I'm afraid so. The chief inspector laughed at the idea that the lord mayor could be involved. He accused me of using my time off to drink and told me that if I get in the way of his bust tonight or do anything to discredit the service, he would ensure I never got my job back. He did let slip that the ritual is somewhere in Rainham, though. They will capture them all tonight, you can be sure of that, but if you want to prove the lord mayor is involved, you'll have to do it yourself.'

'Alright then?' I looked around the room. 'Who's up for a party?'

Party Crashers

Ivor Biggun's house in Chislehurst, a good thirty minute drive from mine, was a gaudy, ugly mix of styles that stood out among the nearby properties like a rhinoceros at a penguin only club. Mock Tudor features clashed with neon signs and the front lawn was dotted with six-foot-tall light-up pink phalluses. Looking the part upon arrival wasn't difficult as we emptied my garage and went there in three Ferrari's and the Lamborghini.

What I hadn't realised when I agreed to go, was that the party goers were expected to be in their underwear. I probably should have seen it coming; the party was at the house of a man who made his money running internet pornography sites. The party would be filled with scantily clad young men and women and people with money. Under any other circumstances you could not have persuaded me to even drive past the place. Tonight though, determined to catch the lord mayor when he left to join the ritual, which I was sure he would, I was going to a porn party in my knickers and bra.

In truth, I wore a negligee because it covered far more of my lumps and bumps and showed the parts I was less embarrassed about revealing. Above all, it covered my stomach because I had to stand next to Barbie whose tight, toned wall of abdominal muscle was just unfair to other women. Over the negligee, I wore a faux fur coat in leopard print and beneath it, the biggest pair of hold-it-all-in pants in my drawer. They started just beneath my boobs and went down to my thighs. I was as covered as I could be at an underwear party, but I still felt uncomfortable.

Mike politely declined the offer to come with us, electing to replace Big Ben at the stakeout of Anthony Perkins. Jane had left because she had another case to pursue for the Blue Moon Investigation Agency, but Jermaine, Big Ben, Tempest, and Barbie came with me and all four of them looked great almost naked since none of them carried more than a trace of body fat.

As we drove up the long driveway to Ivor Biggun's house, heads turned to see the four immaculate Italian sports cars coming their way. We followed a pair of squat caterer's vans onto the property and had to wait in line for them to be directed onwards. It gave me time to look at the venue. The front door was open, light and noise spilling out from within, a heavy bass beat loud enough to make me think the house would vibrate from it.

Two young men in loin cloths and bow ties greeted the lead car driven by Tempest and directed him to a parking area. People who had recently parked their cars were walking back along a carpet to the house, women in nothing but underwear were tottering along in crazy high heels, a hand being held by their man or their friend for balance. It was a crazy sight, but moments later, we were also parked, and it was time to start our search for David Sebastian.

Big Ben looked to be in his element. He wore a body builder's posing pouch, an item of clothing so small I estimated that I could roll it up and hide it inside my belly button. Walking toward the house, he pulled several poses, showing off some impressive muscles which bulged and shifted beneath his skin. Cameramen, whether they were hired in to capture images for the party or were sent there by some tacky tabloid press, I couldn't tell, started snapping shots and encouraging us to smile and pose.

One asked Barbie to take her top off which she politely declined, much to the cameraman's surprise.

'But this is what you do, luv,' he said. 'Your line of work has you naked all day long. Come on, just pop 'em out.'

Realising her error, but unwilling to just pop anything out, she lied, 'I'm one of the makeup girls actually. I don't do the acting.'

'Get a load of me, boys,' yelled Big Ben as he lifted Barbie into the air and held her above his head one handed. He had a sort of Statue of Liberty pose with Barbie held aloft as the flaming torch. Her eyes filled with momentary panic at being nearly nine feet in the air but smiled, nonetheless.

Big Ben put her down and, suitably distracted from asking any further questions by the next group coming up behind us, we slipped inside the house. I had my eyes half shut expecting to see people in the adult film industry shooting live scenes right in front of me, but there was nothing like that going on. To my surprise, it was quite a placid affair; waitresses in naughty maids' outfits were going around with trays of champagne, and everyone was mostly naked, but essential parts were covered and people were just chatting as if it were a semi-formal get together.

Just inside the door was a reception where we handed in the fake invites and had our names checked against a list Jane had put us on less than two hours earlier. They offered to take my coat, though I declined; not only was it keeping me warm, it made me feel like I had some clothes on. Looking around, though, I didn't feel exposed in the way I expected to. Because everyone was wearing less than me, it wasn't much different from being at the pool in a bikini.

As they checked our names against the database, Tempest asked, 'Is David Sebastian here already?'

The man, another one wearing a loin cloth, clicked a few keys and nodded his head. 'Yes, he got here a short while ago.' Okay, that was stage one complete. We were in and the target was here.

Then, a young lady with breasts so fake they looked like balloons, held up a sheet of sticky labels and a marker pen. 'I need your names, stage names that is, not your real ones.'

I hadn't noticed until now, but everyone in the room wore a sticker on their left breast which showed their name.

'Um. I'm Barbie,' said Barbie.

'B-A-R-B-I-E,' the young woman sighed as she spelt it out while she wrote it. 'You're the fifth Barbie tonight.' Looking bored, she peeled off the sticker and handed it over. 'Has anyone got anything original?'

Big Ben thrust his head over the top of me to say, 'Big Ben. Got any of those here tonight?'

'No,' she replied, looking impressed. 'That's actually quite a fun play on words. Well done you.'

Tempest went next, looking a little embarrassed when he said, 'Tommy Salami.'

The woman handed him a sticker. 'Welcome, Tommy.'

Then she pointed the marker at Jermaine, my ever staid and sombre butler. I couldn't tell if he was embarrassed or not, or whether he had to think a name up on the spot or somehow knew one, but he calmly replied, 'The Shlong Ranger.'

He got a sticker too and the marker was thrust at me. What was I supposed to say? I had no idea what a good adult film star name might be and had been feverishly trying to come up with something for the last minute.

'Come on, sweetie. There's a queue forming.' I glanced to my left to see that there was indeed a queue behind me now as they waited for me to move on so they could get inside and enjoy the party.

'Um, I'm Ivana …'

'Speak up, sweetie. I can't hear you with the music in the background.'

'Hurry up!' yelled someone from further down the line.

I could feel my cheeks starting to burn as I swallowed and tried again, this time forcing myself to say it loud enough for everyone to hear. 'Ivana Dickens.'

The woman looked at me for a second, her jaw hanging open, then she dropped the sheet of stickers and the marker. 'Oh, my God! You are my hero. When I first saw you in *Ivana Goes all Night*, I knew I had to follow in your footsteps. You were so influential to so many of us working now. Are you acting again? You barely seem to have aged at all. You look amazing for a woman in her late sixties.'

'Um, thank you?' I replied, unsure what the right answer was and unsure what was happening. It seemed that I had inadvertently chosen a made-up name that belonged to an adult film actress from a few years ago. Thankfully, or not, I looked enough like her to not be called out.

Suddenly, I had people crowding around me, both sexes wanting to pose for pictures with me or shake my hand. I had no idea who the real Ivana Dickens was but everyone else knew her and what she had done. She was famous in this circle.

As the hubbub faded a little, the crowd parted to reveal a man in his late sixties. With a rug of chest hair and a pot belly above thin legs, he rushed towards us. I was certain he had seen Barbie and was going to offer her a part in his next production. Of all the women here, and there were a lot, she was the one that stood out and she was getting a lot of angry looks from other scantily clad girls as she went by.

We were still in the large entrance lobby area, our plan to break up and search the place for David Sebastian yet to be enacted. The man had a thick cigar sticking out of his mouth, sunglasses that hid his eyes, and a large gold ring on every finger. Chest hair man didn't want Barbie though, he wanted me.

'Oh, my goodness, Ivana! I had no idea you were coming tonight. It's so good to see you again after so many years. How are you keeping? You will be perfect for my next movie. Are you with an agent already?' he asked looking around. 'I need to sign you up right now. Come and meet some of my other actors.'

Big Ben loomed over me as he reached for the man's arm. I thought he was going to steer him away, but he grabbed his hand and began pumping it. 'Ivor Biggun, as I live and breathe. What an honour it is to meet you.' It was the host addressing me and Big Ben had dived in to rescue me before I could expose my ignorance and demonstrate that we were party crashers.

'Well, thank you, young man. I must say you have all the makings of a fine actor yourself. Who are you currently working for, I know you are not in my stable of studs?'

Playing along, Big Ben said, 'I'm freelance and just breaking into the industry. I go by the name of Big Ben.' He pointed to the label on his chest.

Just behind Ivor's left shoulder was a man in his late twenties. Tall and muscular, he clearly was one of Ivor's studs, a term I simply hated, but he was eyeing Big Ben with a sneer and when he heard Big Ben announce his

124

stage name, he laughed. 'Big Ben? What utter rubbish.' Big Ben narrowed his eyes at the man. 'You'll never get anywhere with a silly name like that.'

Big Ben turned to Tempest and raised an eyebrow in question. Tempest inclined his head slightly and I wondered what was happening until Big Ben hit the man. It was one punch, his right arm lancing out at lightning speed to collide with his jaw. The man, whose name tag read Lance A Lot, stood looking dazed for a few seconds and then slumped to the floor.

'Be polite,' Big Ben said to the unconscious form before turning his attention back to Ivor. 'Now, Ivor, I'm hoping you can help me locate someone in this grand palace of yours. I need to speak with David Sebastian, the Lord Mayor of Kent. Do you, by chance, happen to know where he is?'

Ivor's eyes were bugging out of his head at Big Ben's display, but he definitely didn't want to refuse to answer the giant man's question. 'He's out by the pool, I think,' he blurted. It wasn't an approach I would have taken, but Big Ben's method delivered us a location for David Sebastian without any of us having to look for him.

Wasting no further time, we moved through the house as a group, heading away from the front door and the lobby toward the back where I assumed the garden and pool would be. I spotted the light coming from it soon enough and there was quite a crowd there already; too many for us to be able to easily identify the man we wanted, and many of the party goers were a lot taller than the lord mayor – he could easily be standing behind someone and we would not be able to see him.

'Let's split up and circle around,' suggested Jermaine, his idea the same one I think we were all having.

Before I picked a direction to go, I spotted a face I knew and froze. 'Jermaine,' I hissed, getting everyone's intention though it was my butler I needed.

'Yes, madam?' he saw where I was looking and followed my eyes to the target so I didn't have to point.

'Is that him?' I asked.

'He who?' asked Barbie.

Jermaine nodded. 'Yes, I think so.'

To answer the question everyone needed an answer to, I said, 'That's James Whitmore. He's the one who dropped his wallet at Mortice Keys shop earlier today and he is very definitely in the cult.'

Tempest asked, 'He's the guy who got a replacement for the ceremonial knife I took?'

'That is my assumption. I didn't see what he took, but the display case the knives were in had been emptied and he had a sack full of things.'

James Whitmore was wearing a pair of bright yellow budgie-smuggler briefs and stood in a group of about fifteen men and women of different ages. Someone said something funny and the group laughed, James moved to his side and there, in the middle of them, was David Sebastian, holding his audience enraptured with an amusing anecdote.

Big Ben started forward, but Tempest grabbed his arm. Big Ben protested, 'I'm just going to knock a few of them out, Tempest. I bet they'll tell me where the missing women are when I start pulling their ears off. Then maybe I can get to know some of the rather lovely ladies here.'

Tempest said, 'Not just yet.' Then he looked about at the other people we could see. 'David Sebastian is here and so is that guy and if one is in the cult then so must the other be. To my mind, seeing the lord mayor here with a man we know to be part of the cult just about closed the case, but I have to question how many other people here are with them?'

Everyone suddenly realised what he was saying, there were hundreds of people here and any of them might be involved.

'We could be surrounded by the very people we are searching for,' said Barbie, her eyes as wide as saucers.

Jermaine added, 'And if we try to snatch the lord mayor, we could find ourselves badly outnumbered very quickly.'

It was a daunting thought, but I had another question, 'Why are they here?' My friends all turned toward me. 'I mean, if they are planning to raise a pagan god tonight and sacrifice several women to do it, haven't they got better things to do than go to a party? I can't work out why they would come here.'

'It is confusing,' Tempest agreed. 'Perhaps they believe they are being watched and are trying to throw people off their scent. They know they were seen at the shop. It might just be paranoia and these two are the only cult members present.'

'But they must have accepted the invitations weeks ago. It feels misleading.' I pursed my lips and tried to think my way through the evidence I could see. 'I feel that I must have missed something vital. I ...' I stopped myself and thought about what clues we had investigated and discarded. 'I can't help but wonder if the concentrated hydrogen peroxide that was on the knife actually meant something.'

Tempest and Big Ben exchanged a look. Big Ben asked, 'You say it was CHP on the knife?'

'Yes. It's an everyday chemical found in thousands of household products.' He and Tempest looked concerned. 'What did I miss?'

It was Tempest who provided the answer. 'CHP is also used as an oxidizer in homemade bombs and I just worked out what the chemistry set at Telelift was for. They weren't cooking crystal meth, they were cooking triacetone triperoxide.'

'Or maybe ethylene glycol dinitrate,' suggested Big Ben.

Tempest didn't argue. 'Either way, there's a distinct possibility we have wandered into something even bigger than a few murders. We could be looking at a terrorist incident.'

Barbie sounded justifiably worried when she asked, 'What do we do?'

I felt very glad to be on my own for this case. Closing it successfully probably wouldn't have been possible without the help of the Blue Moon boys, but since they were here, I needed their help. 'You three gentlemen have to scour this place. I wanted to know why they were here tonight when they ought to be at the ritual, now I worry that I have my answer.'

Jermaine understood. 'The lady at his office said she found the invitation surprising because he tried to have Ivor's sites shut down.'

'And he failed,' I murmured as all the little dots lined up.

Jermaine finished my sentence, 'So he's here to succeed this time by blowing them all to kingdom come.' We were all looking at each other, each of us horrified by the potential of our suspicion.

Then the spell broke when Big Ben slapped Jermaine on his shoulder. He started back toward the building. 'Come on, fellas, we better make sure and then do what we can to clear the place.'

'No, you can't!' I jumped in front of them before they could hurry away. 'If they know the guests are leaving, they might trigger it before they can escape.'

'We have to warn people if there is a bomb here, Patty.' I knew Barbie was right, but we were going to have to do it carefully, nonetheless.

Tempest started toward the house. 'Let's prove there is something to worry about first. Look for a basement or wine cellar.' Tempest, Big Ben, and Barbie were hurrying, their pace fast, but not running so they wouldn't draw attention.

Jermaine remained at my side as I knew he would. 'What do you plan to do, madam?'

In reply, I made a snarling face. 'I'm going on the offensive.'

We had been on the back foot since I got the email from Jerry Brock and my tolerance had worn thin. The ringleader, so far as I could see, was David Sebastian and he was standing six yards from me, holding court.

He saw me coming, but he could not have looked more pleased to see me. 'Patricia! My goodness, what are you doing here? I had no idea you would be on the guest list.'

'Who's Patricia?' said a fake-breasted twenty-something standing next to him. She jabbed a finger in my direction. 'That's Ivana Dickens.'

'Oh, my God, so it is!' said her friend and it started a ripple of attention all coming in my direction. The stupid sticker was confusing people. I tore it off and grabbed David's hand to take him to one side.

An idea occurred to me right then that I hadn't considered before; impulsively, I acted. Still holding David's hand, I crooked a finger to draw Jermaine closer and whispered my plan to him. David had a bemused look on his face when I turned back to him, but he hadn't tried to release my hand. Jermaine, understanding my needs from the few whispered words had already departed which left David and me surrounded by people, yet also separate from them, so we could speak privately.

I tried for a demure look. 'David, I want to thank you for my flowers. They were quite surprising.'

He raised an eyebrow. 'But earlier you said ...' he stopped talking because I was kissing his mouth. My free hand was flat against his chest and my body was pressed against his.

When I broke the kiss a second or so later, his expression had shifted from surprised to confused, but also visible was a smile. 'I bet you don't get much chance for intimacy, do you David?' It was a rhetorical question. 'As a politician you don't get to have casual dalliances or relationships that might go sour and blow up in your face.' He shrugged his agreement, but I yanked his hand and pulled him along behind me. 'I think it's time you and I changed that. My butler is finding us somewhere private where we can … get to know each other.'

Being pulled along behind me, as I wove my way through the press of people, David said, 'Wow. Patricia are you sure about this? I mean, I thought we might make a handsome couple, you and I, but I expected some courtship.'

'No time,' I replied over my shoulder with an embarrassed smile. 'I want you now.'

I could see the excitement in his eyes as I pulled him into the house and spotted Jermaine. Taller than most, his head was visible at the far end of the room where he waited for me. Crossing the room with David still in tow and his hand still holding mine, Jermaine went back through the door and into a wide hallway. I hadn't been in this part of the house yet, but I didn't need to know where I was or where I was going, I trusted Jermaine completely. He reached a door and held it open for me to pass him and go inside. I shot one quick glance at David as I went through the door, both to reassure him and to make sure his eyes were on me and not Jermaine who wrapped a huge arm around David's neck.

I finally got my hand back as David let it go and bucked against his assailant. I knew it would only take Jermaine a few seconds; the sleeper hold interrupting the flow of blood to the lord mayor's brain and preventing him from yelling for help.

I got in his face. 'Did you really think I wouldn't work it out. You went to school with Mortice Keys. It was there for anyone to see. Once you add

Anthony Perkins to the list it was ridiculously arrogant of you to think you could go ahead with the ritual tonight. You must have known we would work it out once we had his car. You're going to jail, lord mayor.'

I had no time to say anything more because his eyes had already rolled back. Jermaine dragged the limp body into the room, a small office of some kind, and laid him on the carpet. I had sent him in ahead of me with a simple instruction to find a lockable room. If the pagans knew David was inside, they wouldn't blow the building up. At least, that was my belief. It would give us a little longer to prove the theory that they were making explosives and that David planned to blow the place up to settle a score.

Jermaine ripped the cord from a printer and used it to tie the lord mayor's hands and feet while I stuffed a few tissues into his mouth and ran a tape dispenser around and around his head and then around his ankles and wrists for good measure. Then we tied him to a desk. He wouldn't be out for long, but it would give us the chance to find Tempest and the others and evacuate the party if necessary.

'I think that should do it, madam,' said Jermaine standing back to check our handywork. 'Do you not wish to interrogate him?'

David's eyes fluttered open, consciousness returning after less than a minute. It took him about a second to get his bearings before his eyes filled with panic. He struggled and bucked but the oak desk had to weigh four hundred pounds – it wasn't going anywhere. He knew he was caught, and all his plans were going up in smoke.

I thought about Jermaine's question but shook my head. 'Anyone who is crazy enough to be sacrificing people to a pagan god is going to be filled with the kind of insane fervour that doesn't answer questions. He believes that what he is doing is right. A bit like Angelica Howard-Box in many ways but she doesn't feel a need to cut out hearts.'

David's eyes were going wild as he tried to get free. I knelt next to him. 'We'll be back soon. First we need to find the explosives you planted here and save all the people.' His eyes widened in alarm. 'Yes, I'm sorry' my apology dripping with irony. 'Every part of your plan is about to unravel.'

Then without another word, Jermaine and I left him tied to the desk. As we went out the door, he was still struggling to get free though I didn't think he could, and I happily closed the door on him as I dialled Barbie on my phone.

It rang but it wasn't answered. I tried again with the same result. As dread filled my stomach, I phoned Tempest and felt my panic beginning to rise when that too didn't reach anyone. So when, just as it had to be about to click over to voicemail, it was suddenly answered, I felt a wave of relief and had to put a hand to my heart.

'Oh, Tempest!' I exclaimed. 'I was starting to worry something had happened.'

There was a heartbeat of silence at the other end. Then a man who wasn't Tempest said. 'You're too late.'

As adrenalin flooded into my body, making me feel sick and weak, I managed to stammer. 'We have your high priest. We know who you are, and we are coming for you. If you hurt my friends ...'

I didn't know how to finish my threat, but I didn't get a chance to. The voice said, 'You don't know anything at all, and no one is going to stop us.' Then the line went dead.

Jermaine had been close enough to hear the whole thing and now he grabbed my arm, heading to a window where he had seen something. Outside in the dark, James Whitmore and others were getting into cars and a small truck with the caterer's logo on the side was just rolling out of the gate.

'They must have them,' he said, meaning Barbie and the guys. 'We have to get after them,' he growled in his anger. Already moving toward the front of the house so he could get to a car and pursue his friends, I had to hold him back.

When his eyes met mine, I knew he could see the apology in them. 'We have to save these people first. There might be a bomb here.' He grimaced, unable to present an argument, knowing I was right, but fearful for his friend anyway. Then he closed his eyes and centred himself, a thing I had seen him do several times before and generally just before he unleashed a whole world of hurt on someone.

When he reopened them, he was calm. 'If they brought explosives here, they would need to have been disguised as something else. Or hidden somewhere in the house a while ago. Tempest was looking for a basement.'

I followed his train of thought. 'We need to short cut this. We don't have the time to search the house, let's ask the owner.' I didn't know where Ivor Biggun was and there was altogether too much house to search, so I started yelling. 'Ivor Biggun!'

Jermaine joined in. 'Ivor Biggun!' We ran through the house, yelling like banshees until we found him. Alerted by our shouts, he was coming our way. The man Big Ben floored was back on his feet and with him still, as were a small entourage of other men and women, lured by the noise Jermaine and I were making.

Seeing me making a beeline for him, Ivor asked, 'What is going on, Ivana? Is everything okay?'

I waved a hand in his face to shut him up, grabbing his elbow to steer him away from his followers. 'Firstly, my name isn't Ivana. I am not some tired porn star from the eighties making some ridiculous comeback. My name is Patricia Fisher, I'm a private investigator and I came here tonight to solve a crime. Does your house have a basement?'

Ivor couldn't keep up with the information being thrown at him. 'Wait, what? Ivana, I'm confused.'

'Yes, you are,' I agreed. 'I'm not Ivana, but that's not important. Does your house have a basement?'

'No. No, it doesn't.' He tried to ask me why I had asked and why I wanted to know, but my brain was racing now. Tempest and the others had been snatched, which increased the likelihood that there was a bomb here and they were grabbed because they disturbed the bombers.

Then it hit me. 'The caterers!' I yelled at Jermaine. 'What are caterers doing here at this time? The party is well under way. All the food and drink should have been delivered hours ago. Why are there vans here now?'

He started running, seeing the truth of it and knowing what it must mean.

I got a, 'Hey!' as I ran after my butler. Ivor, befuddled by my actions, chose to follow me and his entourage followed him. By the time I caught up with Jermaine in the garden, there had to be more than one hundred people trailing behind me.

There was a caterer's van parked against the side of the house.

Ivor Biggun said, 'That's not the catering firm I use.'

Jermaine opened the back, the roller door shooting up to the roofline. Inside the van were dozens of blue plastic barrels. Into the top of each one was a fat cable and each of them came from an electronic box. I didn't need to climb inside to see that it was a bomb and neither did anyone else.

Small squeals of panic were coming from behind me as Ivor Biggun's guests began to back away. It opened a floodgate as word spread, party goers running to get away causing more of those inside to question what was happening. In seconds it became a stampede and I started to hear car engines starting up, immediately followed by the squeal of tyres and honking of horns as hundreds of people left the party as one terrified mass.

'We should leave too, madam,' advised Jermaine, stepping away from the van. 'It might also be a pertinent time to call the police.'

'Yes,' I murmured, digging for my phone in the pocket of my faux fur jacket. 'We have to get the lord mayor too.'

I called the number I was quite certain would answer; that of Chief Inspector Quinn. 'Good evening, Mrs Fisher. I do hope you are calling to arrange turning yourself in. You do not seem well-suited to life on the run. If you have an explanation for smashing your way into a shop in Canterbury, then it will be taken into account.'

'Nevermind all that nonsense, Chief Inspector. There is a bomb at Ivor Biggun's house, and I have the lord mayor in custody.'

'The lord mayor! Have you lost your senses, woman? What are you doing with the lord mayor?'

'Chief Inspector, did you miss the part about the bomb?'

'How do you know there is a bomb?'

Jermaine and I were weaving our way back through the house to get to David Sebastian. The bomb had been a hunch until we found it and I really wasn't convinced they wouldn't blow the place up with him in it. Maybe they didn't even know he was in the house, but even if they did, they had proven themselves bloodthirsty. Was it entirely unlikely one might feel a promotion to high priest was available if they pressed the button and created a job opening?

'Chief inspector, the ceremonial knife had CHP on it and Anthony Perkins, the man whose car I crashed at the ritual last night, has a chemistry lab set up at his business address. That's just circumstantial,' I added quickly before he could. 'The van filled with barrels rigged to a detonator, is what gives it away for me. It's backed up against the side of Ivor Biggun's house. Now get off your fat backside, stop wasting time, and mobilise the bomb squad!' I was shouting by the time I reached the end of my reply, but not just to get my point across. Mostly, it was driven by desperate frustration because I was looking at the oak desk and David Sebastian was no longer there.

137

The beep for call waiting sounded in my ear. I moved the phone so I could see the screen just as Chief Inspector Quinn began to respond, but I cut him off when I saw the name displayed. 'Sorry, Chief Inspector, I have someone important on the other line.'

'Mike, give me good news,' I begged.

His voice was quiet when he replied. 'Anthony Perkins just left his place. I am tailing him. It's too early to guess where he is going, but he is driving in the general direction of West Malling which means he is going in the opposite direction to where Chief Inspector Quinn believes the ritual is taking place. Where are you?'

I didn't answer for a few seconds, long enough for Mike to prompt me anyway. I was on my knees looking at the neatly cut Sellotape. Someone had found our captive and set him free. Just like Cinderella, he was going to the ball. There might even be dancing to go along with the human sacrifice he had planned. 'Mike, sorry. There's a bomb at Ivor Biggun's house, it's all to do with David Sebastian. He has some kind of vendetta against him so planned to use his contacts to make explosives which he would then use to kill or maim half the people at the party.'

Mike swore. 'I have to get the bomb squad over there.'

Jermaine and I had made it outside. The car parking area was almost devoid of cars, but my three Ferrari's and the Lamborghini were still there. Between us we could have taken two, but I wasn't worried about saving cars when lives were on the line so we both aimed for the bright red 360 Spider. I had to hope everyone was out because I wasn't going back inside to conduct a room by room search. Hurrying toward my car, I told Mike, 'I think the area is clear of people and I just told Chief Inspector Quinn. I'm not sure he listened, but his taskforce is heading to the wrong address. He has been getting misled from the start.' I fell silent again as my skull itched. He *had* been getting misled from the start, but what did that mean? I was at my car but still needed to get further away from the house. 'Mike, I've got to go. Let me know where Perkins goes. We need the location of that ceremony.' I swallowed before delivering the bad news. 'Mike, they've got Barbie, and they took Tempest and Big Ben too.'

He swore again and I heard him huff out a determined breath. 'I'll let you know as soon as I have something.'

As he hung up, I reconnected my call to Chief Inspector Quinn who I was surprised to find still holding. 'Chief Inspector, are you ready to listen?' I asked, wondering if I might now get through to him, but also aware I was running the risk of alienating myself completely.

'You have thirty seconds, Mrs Fisher. Entertain me with your fanciful tale.' His tone betrayed the anger he felt but I had his ear.

A giant explosion rocked my car, cutting off any possibility that I might speak. A huge fireball shot into the sky and outwards in every direction, carrying with it pieces of the van and Ivor Biggun's house. We were just coming off the drive and into the road when the explosion occurred. The blast wave rocked the car, Jermaine almost losing control as he fought the steering wheel. Then a pair of pink plastic phalluses barrelled across the road in front of us, causing Jermaine to slam on the brakes.

'What was that?' asked the chief inspector.

'You can cancel the bomb squad,' I squeaked, barely able to speak I was so terrified. 'Chief Inspector, you are in the wrong place. Your men will find no one and nothing when you instigate your raid in Rainham. The lord mayor is behind it all and you need to call Mike Atwell, reinstate him, and go to the location he gives you. He is following one of the cult members there now.'

Silence was all I got in response, until, after two seconds, he said, 'I'll look into it.' Then he hung up. He displayed rudeness but it felt like a concession at the same time. He would look into it and would quickly hear that a bomb had gone off. Then he would see that all the things I had told him were true.

In truth, I was praying Mike was being led to the location for the ritual because if not, I had no idea how to find them and I only had a few hours left to work it out.

'Where to, madam?' asked Jermaine.

It was a great question. We couldn't go home; the chance of there being police waiting to arrest me for the break in earlier was too great. Jermaine and I had to remain on the playing board until the game was done. Our destination had to be the pagan ritual. Until we found out where that was, it didn't matter where we went.

I told him, 'Let's head in the general direction of home. Mike said Anthony Perkins is heading that way. Maybe we'll get lucky and the ritual won't be too far away.'

I wanted to call Barbie, just in case she still had her phone and hadn't been able to answer it earlier. Had that been the case, though, she would call me as soon as she was able, so instead, I cursed myself for not making sure David couldn't escape and wished, yet again, that I had packed a bag of clothes so I could cover myself up.

When my phone rang, I almost wet myself. I had it in my hand, but I was still buzzing with adrenalin from kidnapping the lord mayor, discovering my friends were missing and, the bomb going off. Seeing Mike's name on the screen, I took a breath and punched the button to answer it.

Fast as anything I snapped out my questions, 'Mike, have they stopped? Do you know where the ritual is?'

'Oh, God, Patricia I'm so sorry. I just got hit by another car. My car is a wreck. I lost them.'

I started to hyperventilate. With no way to find their location, Barbie and the guys were as good as dead. Trying to keep a lid on the despair I felt, I asked, 'Where were you when you got hit?'

'On the Kings Hill bypass, just before the turnoff to West Malling but I don't know whether they took it or not.' The bypass went from the M20 motorway to Kings Hill but then carried on to Hadlow, Paddock Wood, Tonbridge, and a thousand other places. Anthony Perkins could be going anywhere.

'Are you okay?' My brain was able to function well enough to check if Mike was hurt or not.

'Yes, yes. Patricia. I banged my head; it is hardly significant. Quinn called me, I guess you talked to him. He actually sounded like he had some doubts about his plan for once. He is waiting for me to confirm the location of the ritual though. Hold on, the other chaps are getting out of their car, I think they want to exchange insurance details.' Then he swore for the third time this evening but this time he wasn't venting his frustration; I could tell the difference. Now he had a problem. 'Patricia, can you send a squad car to the bypass please, just east of the West Malling turn off. The car that hit me wasn't an accident. It's pagans and they don't look friendly.'

My heart was in my mouth. He was all alone on a dark road and undoubtedly outnumbered. 'Mike?' I squealed.

'Find the ceremony, Patricia, save your friends.' Then his phone went dead as my head filled with images of him trying to fight off a carful of men.

I dialled three nines and screamed my message at the dispatcher. I hadn't recognised the voice when she spoke, but I wasn't really listening and had blood thumping through my head as yet another of my friends fell foul to a murderous cult. She recognised me though, 'Patricia is that you? It's Patience Woods, what's occurring girl, you sound like you're in trouble. Hey, you know there's a warrant out for your arrest?'

I first met Police Constable Patience Woods last week while investigating a different case. She knew Tempest through his girlfriend who was also his partner at the Blue Moon Investigation Agency. I cannot express how good it felt to hear a friendly voice. 'Patience, there's not much time to explain. Mike Atwell has just been attacked by cult members, the same group who killed Gerard Gallagher and who were going to kill Linda Cole last night out in Newington. He's on the West Malling bypass where they ran him off the road, but it's much worse than that.'

'Keep it coming, girl,' she snapped her reply. I could hear a flurry of activity in the background and lots of voices as I imagined other dispatchers crowding around her station – one of their own was in trouble and they would rally to save him.

'It's Tempest and Big Ben,' I told her. 'The cult have them too.'

'Big Ben? They have my man?'

I didn't know if the two of them were together or not. It seemed like an unlikely pairing, but I wasn't going to get into that now. 'They also have Barbie, my blonde friend. If they are not already dead, then they will kill them soon enough. You have to get someone to Mike's location.'

143

'Where are the others?' Patience asked, desperate to know.

'I don't know,' I wailed. 'Mike was tailing one of the very few cult members we managed to identify when they hit him. They must have spotted him watching the house but that could mean anything. They could have been leading him away from the ritual or maybe they spotted him just before they got to it. I just don't know.'

A new voice spoke to me, 'Hello, this is Sergeant Butterworth. We are dispatching several cars to the location you have given us for DS Atwell. Now, I want you to give me your location, or turn yourself over, Mrs Fisher. I understand you think you are pursuing a case, but you do not have the authority to break into premises in so doing. Only the police have that authority.'

'My friends have been grabbed by a cult of pagan god worshippers responsible for at least one murder, you idiot.' I raged.

Sergeant Butterworth wasn't to be dissuaded. 'Chief Inspector Quinn is leading a taskforce that will capture the cult members shortly. Now turn yourself in, Mrs Fisher. It will go better for you than us having to chase you down.'

I told him exactly what he could do with his demands and screamed for him to put Patience back on the line. I didn't believe he would, so I pulled my phone from my ear to jab the button to end the call. The last thing I heard before the line went dead was his question, 'Where did Woods go?'

I just couldn't believe the situation I found myself in. We were going to lose, and we were going to lose big time. The police would arrest the lord mayor tomorrow and it would all come out, all the gory details and they would arrest all of his fellow cult members, identifying them one at a time perhaps, but by then it would be too late. Much too late to save Barbie and Mike. Too late to save Tempest and Big Ben and far too late for Helena Gallagher and the other captives.

Neither Jermaine nor I spoke for the next few minutes. We were still heading home from Ivor Biggun's house but nearing the M20 motorway which we would cross to find ourselves on the Kings Hill bypass. There was a distinct chance there would be police there and they might know enough about me to stop the red Ferrari just in case.

I wasn't sure I cared anymore. Constantly trying to think my way around the problem, I was mired in a pit of despair and wallowing in grief I believed I would soon feel.

My phone rang. I didn't know the number, but I answered it anyway, half expecting it to be a cult member at the other end calling to gloat.

'Patricia Fisher,' I managed as a tear rolled down my face. At the last second, I told myself it might be a customer, so I had to act as if the sun would come up tomorrow.

A croaky whisper came back at me. 'Mrs Fisher, this is Frank.'

'Frank?'

'Yes, Frank Decaux, the bookshop owner?'

The dots aligned in my head. 'Sorry, Frank this really isn't a good time. Can you call back later?' I went to stab the red button on my phone, but his voice stopped me.

'No, wait! I've been trying to call Tempest and Big Ben, but I couldn't get a response from them. Now I know why; the pagans have them!'

'Wait,' I shot forward in my seat, sitting bolt upright as I dared to hope. 'How do you know that?'

'Because I'm with the pagans and I can see them!' he squeaked. 'I figured if the world was about to end under the fiery boot of Quentiox freshly raised to life through the pagan high priest, then I might as well die trying to stop it happening.'

Oh, my word! Tempest told me the man had the heart of a lion; he had infiltrated their group and was with them now. 'Frank, where are you? I can bring reinforcements.' I held my breath as I waited for his reply.

'St Leonard's Tower.'

'St ... but that's less than a mile from my house!'

'Listen, it's all about to start happening here. The high priest is talking to the audience, whipping them into a frenzy. I'm here with Poison. We are going to try to kill him. They will kill us the moment we do but if we save the world ...'

'No, Frank,' I squealed, trying to get through to the undoubtedly brave but definitely crazy man. 'I'm coming. The police are coming. Just give me a little time. Can you do that? You said they would do the sacrifices at midnight. That gives me more than two hours. You have to give me long enough to get there.'

'I'll do what I can, but I won't let the world end when I could have stopped it. Have them name a library after me,' he whispered. Then he ended the call and I could only imagine what he might do if we didn't get there in time.

We had a location! That was the key point, now I just needed to get the word out.

The very next second, the darkness all around us was filled with flashing red and blue as a squad car gave us lights and sirens. It had snuck up behind us when we were listening intently to Frank.

'Not now,' snarled Jermaine, stomping down on the gas. The Ferrari took off so fast I though we might accelerate off the side of the planet. One moment he was obeying the speed limit and trundling along at fifty, the next time my heart beat we were doing a hundred and twenty and still gaining speed.

He tore up the bypass, flashing past a pair of squad cars parked next to Mike's abandoned car. The turning for West Malling came and went but we were going too fast to consider turning anyway. About two miles ahead of us, the two-lane highway narrowed to one and he would have to slow, it also terminated at a roundabout with a set of lights. He could ignore the lights; we were running from the law after all, but the flashing lights from the squad car were soon lost to the darkness behind us and he slowed to take the roundabout at a speed that wouldn't kill us.

The next roundabout, just a quarter of a mile from the first, gave us the option of heading into West Malling from the other direction and it would take us right in front of St Leonard's Tower.

The Tower is an ancient remnant of a larger building, but it was so old that no one knew why it had been built or what its original purpose might have been. The road into West Malling ran straight by it but the grounds extended a mile beyond the road and could easily hide a gathering like the pagans wanted for their ritual. Even with torches lit, no one would see them from the road and there were no houses close enough to notice anything occurring.

'You're heading to the tower?' I asked Jermaine.

'Yes, madam. With your permission, I intend to hurt some people.'

'Permission granted. I think I have a better idea though. We just need to make a small stop.' I also needed to make one more phone call. Chief Inspector Quinn wanted a location before he would commit to sending officers. Well, now I had one. As the call connected, I ran through what I was going to have to do. The police wouldn't get here for at least thirty minutes, not in large enough numbers. A handful might see it as their duty to tackle the pagans anyway, but I worried they would just become another statistic, or yet more hostages.

Just as Chief Inspector Quinn's voice echoed in my ear, I made my decision. Now it would come down to how convincing I could be.

The Church Council

My plan was as ridiculous as it was simple. Unfortunately, I also relied, to some extent, on the goodwill and trust of a woman who offered me neither. I discussed it with Jermaine.

'Do you believe it will work, madam?' he asked.

'If I can get Angelica Howard-Box on my side, the rest will follow. I might not like her, but she controls the other council members.'

'Very good, madam.'

Jermaine parked the Ferrari next to a large silver Mercedes. I was dressed like a harlot, I was going to sound like an insane woman, and I had absolutely no choice about my current course of action. This was going to work. At least, that's what I had been telling myself for the last two minutes as Jermaine threaded his way around the country lanes to get to the village hall.

I had to clamber to get out of the low-slung car in a dignified manner, but I managed it, tottering on my silly heels because they were all I had to wear.

Jermaine, still wearing next to nothing himself despite the dropping night temperature outside, offered me his arm to escort me inside.

The conversation stopped dead the second I got through the door.

Yet again, Angelica Howard-Box was lording it over everyone else in the room, standing when everyone else was sitting, and following her clipboard of agenda points. Now she was staring open-mouthed at me as the other members of the church council turned my way to see what held her attention.

Wing Commander Roy Hope, a retired RAF fighter pilot who had flown in the Falkland Islands war in the early eighties, was now a jolly man in his sixties with a red face and a thin covering of snowy white hair. Seeing me, he laughed. 'Hey, reverend, you didn't say there was a tarts and vicars party afterwards!'

As he continued to chuckle, Angelica folded her arms and scowled at me. 'What is the meaning of this, Patricia? I kicked you off the church council, remember?'

'Yes, Angelica. You still don't have the authority to do that, you power-mad cow.' Her eyes bugged right out of her head at my insult and I could see she was winding up a retort.

Jermaine leaned his head down to whisper in my ear. 'Madam, your plan was to win her over.'

I smiled. 'Plan B.' Striding to the centre of the room and passing between the seated council members, I started talking. 'If you want to know why I am dressed like this ...'

'You look like a slut,' spat Angelica.

Ignoring her, mostly because she was right, I continued, 'I was undercover on a case investigating the recent disappearance of several people. One of them was found murdered in a pagan ritual forty-eight hours ago.' Gasps rang out and half the people seated before me crossed themselves. 'There is a pagan cult operating in this area and they are planning to murder several more people tonight.'

Angelica sighed dramatically. 'Oh, Patricia, you do have a theatrical imagination. Pagans murdering people. You should get your facts straight. The pagans worship earth gods, they are peaceful and giving. They want to eat of the Earth and give back to mother nature. What are you suggesting? Human sacrifice?'

I locked eyes with the vicar. 'You studied theology, Geoffrey. What do you say? Are the pagans all peace loving? Or were there other deities in their history who were less inclined to respect the rights of others?'

The reverend Geoffrey Grey had been the parish vicar for as long as I could remember. He had to be nearing retirement now, not that I was sure what age vicars were expected to retire, but his mind was whip fast. 'Yes, Patricia,' he agreed, which garnered a harrumph from Angelica. 'The pagans' history is littered with murderous rituals.'

'Well, one of them is taking place right now at St Leonard's Tower. They have some of my friends, a police officer and several other hostages who they intend to sacrifice.' Announcing that it was so close to them got another ripple of gasps and everyone was talking suddenly, arguing between themselves and looking worried.

'How do you know any of this?' demanded Angelica, still trying to be in charge.

I got to smile when I said, 'I'm a detective.'

It was time to deliver to them the real reason why I was with them. 'Unless you want West Malling to become known as the murder capital of Kent, you need to call everyone in your phone and get them out of their houses. It's a five-minute walk to the tower from here. If we show up in force, we can drive them away and rescue the hostages.'

'Isn't this a job for the police?' asked Angelica, managing to sound bored and frowning at me with a chuckle as if I was just being ridiculous and everyone should see me for the clown that I am.

151

Then the entrance door slammed open and two uniformed cops burst in.

'Oh, thank goodness!' exclaimed Angelica, clapping her hands with joy. 'Now maybe we can end this daft charade and get back to church business.'

She hadn't seen that I was smiling.

'You made that more difficult than it needed to be, babes,' said Patience. 'That Ferrari of yours is fast.'

I face palmed. 'Was that you behind me?' Patience crossed the room, the other cop, a man, coming with her. I realised I knew him too. His name was Hardacre, another constable though in contrast to Patience, he looked ready to arrest me on the spot.

'Damned skippy it was. I put the lights on because I thought you would stop. I only found you here because that fine car is kinda easy to spot.'

'Excuse me,' snarled Angelica, upset about being ignored. 'Shouldn't you be arresting her?'

Patience looked Angelica up and down, then raised her hands to get everyone's attention. 'Ladies and gents, we have a situation and I need your help. There's a pagan ritual about to take place at St Leonard's Tower.'

Angelica threw her clipboard on the floor. 'Oh, for heaven's sake. Vicar I must demand that you evict this ... woman,' she wafted her arm in my direction. 'She is no longer on the church council and has no right to attend this meeting.' Then she jabbed a finger at Patience, a move which I didn't think would get her the response she desired. 'As for you. I happen to know that this woman has an outstanding warrant for her arrest. Now I suggest you get on with it before I call my good friend the chief constable and have you sacked.'

Patience whipped out her right hand to grab Angelica's finger and bent it upwards. Angelica squawked in fright and tried, ineffectually, to snatch her hand away. Patience said, 'That wasn't a very polite way to speak to a police officer, now was it? Hardacre, I believe she threatened me. Do you think snapping her finger off is justifiable?'

He rolled his eyes and intervened. 'No, Patience. Not even nearly.' As PC Hardacre took hold of her arm, Patience let go but made sure Angelica saw that she was watching her.

'Now everyone,' shouted Patience. 'We have a problem and your community needs your help.'

'Wot, ho!' cried the wing commander. 'Let's loose the dogs of war and shout ballyhoo! For God and King George!'

I heard his wife whisper, 'Elizabeth is still on the throne you daft old codger.'

Unsurprisingly, Angelica had more to say. 'Your community does need your help.' Her agreement surprised me until she spoke again. 'It needs your help to rid it of Patricia Fisher and her terrible influence. Did we have pagan rituals before she arrived.'

'I've lived here all my life,' I pointed out.

'Did we have people getting kidnapped and car chases through the high street before she arrived?'

'What car chases?' I asked, screwing my face up at her wild accusations.

Patience stepped in again. 'One more word, lady and I'll put you in the back of the squad car for obstruction of an officer's duty.'

Angelica crossed her arms again. 'You'll do no such thing,' she sounded utterly certain and she looked at Hardacre to reel his colleague in again. 'Go on. Tell her.'

Hardacre narrowed his eyes. 'No, I think PC Woods is about right. Pipe down now, there's a good lady.'

'Well, I ...' Angelica stormed to a table at the side, snatched up her handbag and stormed to the door. 'The chief constable will hear of this!' her voice echoed back as she went outside.

'Right, folks,' said Patience, glad the constant interruptions were at an end. 'This is what I need you to do.'

As she laid out the same plan that I devised, my mind began to wander. There *was* something I had missed. It went right back to the start of the case and it had fundamental implications for every decision I had made today. If I was right, and my itchy skull assured me I was, then it explained why this had been so tough to solve, why David Sebastian's school friends were so successful and why Chief Inspector Quinn was in the wrong place. Now I just had to find the link to prove that I was right, and I knew just the person to do that.

As Patience finished and the council members became a flurry of activity, I made a phone call to Jane Butterworth who answered the phone with a sleepy yawn, became very quickly alert when I told her about Tempest and the others, and then promised to get back to me as soon as she could.

The Mob

The procession heading out of West Malling looked to be fifty yards long and had to have more than a hundred people in it. Patience and her partner, Brad Hardacre, I felt it necessary to learn his name, had thinned the crowd of volunteers down a little when several dads turned up with their kids, some of whom they carried on their shoulders like we were going to a carnival.

It was a healthy number though, assembled in minutes as the small community rallied to the cry for help. Instructed to arm themselves, they came with cricket bats, and garden forks, held aloft to prevent anyone getting accidentally forked in the darkness. The wing commander ducked into his house on the High Street to reappear a moment later with a machine gun.

PC Hardacre promptly confiscated it which left the wing commander with nothing but a walking cane, but he brandished it like a sword nevertheless and jabbed the air with menace.

The two police officers were leading, the ragtag mob following on behind and in great spirits as if they didn't understand what we might face. It was eleven fifteen, but PC Hardacre assured me the cavalry was on its way. Chief Inspector Quinn's taskforce was on route to us right now, but I knew we couldn't afford to wait. If Frank felt he had to act, he would get himself killed. Maybe he would kill the high priest, but he had a young woman with him, he said, Poison going with her boss even though his plan was nuts.

As we approached St Leonard's Tower, I called for quiet, sending a message back through the snaking line of villagers and listening to the hubbub of conversation tail off. The tower loomed ahead but there was no sign that anyone was here. No cars were in sight, but they would have left their vehicles in the country park opposite and walked the last hundred yards to the tower.

I put a hand on Brad's shoulder. 'You're happy with the plan?' I asked.

'Not even slightly, Mrs Fisher. However, I cannot offer an alternative and maybe a show of force will be sufficient to give them pause. We are fast running out of time and CI Quinn just said he is still at least ten minutes from arriving.'

'Don't worry, Patricia,' said the wing commander, sounding gleeful at the prospect of a fight. 'Good will overcome.'

Patience held out her radio. 'Here, you'll be needing this.' I took it, nodded thanks to both the officers and ran the rest of the way up the steep berm I faced. The tower sat behind a natural rise which provided perfect cover for the pagans who wanted to be hidden from the road, but now gave my mob cover from them instead. As long as they stayed quiet, the pagans, and in particular, the high priest, would have no idea they were there. Until I revealed them, that is.

Jermaine held my hand as we crested the bank. In front of us was the crowd of pagans, hidden inside the walls which extended out from the tower. The walls were a thousand years old and had crumbled in places which meant there were lots of easy access and egress points. At the far end as we faced it, the high priest addressed his followers, his voice booming across the ground to keep the pagans enraptured. The crowd faced him, but to his left and right were half a dozen of his senior council, each of them controlling a wooden cage in which a human could be seen. They were trapped in the cages, a shock of blonde hair moving inside one telling me that Barbie was still alive.

'Brethren and sistren, tonight with the blood of these most honoured sacrifices, we will give honour to Quentiox and he will rise!' He got a cheer

158

from the crowd. 'He has granted us the perfect night for us to honour him; cloudless skies so the moon can watch us bathe in the blood of our offerings. Through him, as he ascends once more to rule the Earth this night, we will rise successful among the unaware, those fools who follow their lesser gods. We, the righteous, will ...'

'Ah, shut up, man,' yelled Big Ben from his cage. 'You're boring me.' Big Ben's keeper kicked his cage which elicited some interesting words in response. Followed by, 'When I get out of here, there won't be enough left of your teeth for them to identify your body by dental inspection.'

Uncowed, the man kicked his cage again.

The high priest, interrupted by Big Ben's outburst attempted to restart, but this time, I chose to disrupt the ceremony. 'Hello, everyone.'

When hundreds of heads snapped around to look, it was only me that they saw. Upon my instruction, Jermaine had already departed, using the darkness to make his way around the outside of the wall to a better position.

Now that I had their attention, I waved. No one in the crowd came my way, but from the front by the high priest, two of the pagans minding the cages started running. They planned to deal with me, but I wasn't worried. The answer from Jane had arrived a minute ago and now I knew what I was dealing with.

'Good evening, Albert Brady. Or should I call you chief constable?' I shouted so everyone would hear me. The high priest, whose arms had been held aloft this whole time, dropped them now. He was clearly surprised that I knew who he was. It had been tricky, he was six inches taller now, making him roughly the same height as David Sebastian. But the robe covered his legs completely and I was certain we would find stilts or something attached to his legs.

I smiled at the sea of faces staring up at me. 'Who else is here who doesn't think they will get caught? Anthony Perkins, you must be in here somewhere, Mortice Keys, I can see you,' I lied. I couldn't see him, but he wasn't to know that, and he made himself visible by starting to move toward the edge of the crowd. 'How about James Whitmore, chief strategist to the lord mayor? I bet you're one of the ones at the front.' I had just named the only names I knew, but the susurration of whispers going around the crowd now told me everyone else was waiting for me to say their name and wondering who else knew.

'Enough,' bellowed the high priest, his voice filling the air. 'Grab her. She can join the others.'

The two men from the far end were getting closer now, running along the bank of earth that had formed around the wall. I was standing on a berm of grass covered soil, a high spot which gave me a commanding view but also hid from sight that which I did not want the high priest and the crowd to see. With a glance behind me to my left and right, I nodded and counted down with the fingers of my left hand, talking as I did. I expected the pagans to be a suspicious bunch, so I was going to prey on that and use it to my advantage.

'Quentiox is displeased with you chief constable.'

'I am his high priest!' he roared.

'Really? Who appointed you? Did you appoint yourself?' Like watching a tennis match all the heads swung back around to see what he had to say.

'Quentiox, the goat-headed god came to me in a dream and demanded that I raise an army of followers. Together we would raise him from his grave and reinstate him as the rightful ruler of Earth.'

160

'Then why is he making your loyal followers disappear? I folded in the final finger on my hand just as the two men running at me got within two yards. From the crowds' perspective, they then vanished from sight. From where I was, they got their legs ripped out from under them by two men on each side who were being directed by Patience and Brad. They were then quickly gagged and hogtied by the villagers hidden from sight behind the berm. A ripple of surprise rang out from the crowd.

I was stalling for time. The villagers were poised but I didn't want to endanger anyone. If this turned into a melee, injuries would follow, and I didn't want anyone's death on my conscience. The police were coming, and it still wasn't so close to midnight that I was risking them killing everyone. I just wanted a few more minutes.

I didn't get them though.

In the brief confusion I had caused, the high priest and his followers hadn't noticed two small figures making their way to the front. Just as the high priest pointed to me and yelled, 'Seize her!' an instruction that made the crowd surge my way as one, the two small figures ran in the opposite direction. I knew who they were just because I could see which way they were going, and because I caught a flash of bright pink-coloured hair in the moonlight. Then, as I accepted there was no way to avoid the fight, I saw Jermaine streaking in from the right. He had gone all the way around to pop up level with the cages. There were ten of the pagans left minding the cages, plus the high priest, but when Jermaine drop kicked the first one and hit the release bar, he set Tempest free, and it was suddenly ten against four and the odds improved again when Poison and Frank came in from the other end to surprise the man there. Suddenly Mike was free, and the tide was turning.

'No, you fools!' raged the high priest. 'Don't all go to get her. Some of you come back and defend the offerings.' The ambiguous instruction just turned the crowd around again as they tried to work out which of them should run which way.

'Now?' asked Patience.

With a nervous smile, I replied, 'Yes, I think now would be good.'

The pagans were sorting themselves out but when I looked back to the high priest my eyes came out on stalks. He was in the middle of the line of cages, trying to get one of them open so he could sacrifice the person inside before anyone could stop him. However, to his right, Tempest, Big Ben and Jermaine were going through the guards like they were punching bags set up for a little target practice. A spin kick from Jermaine flung one man in Big Ben's direction where a scything arm felled him like a tree. Coming from the other side, were Mike, Frank, Poison, and now Barbie as they popped her cage open.

Frank was holding a double headed axe! Where the heck he got it from or how he hid it under his robe I might never know, but he never got a chance to use it because Poison was in front of him, her arms a whirling dervish of deadly skill, cracking skulls with a set of nunchucks.

It was just the original honour sacrifices left and one of them would be Helena Gallagher.

Below me, the pagans had finally sorted themselves, so roughly half were rushing back toward the high priest and the other half were surging toward me.

Patience and Brad led the villagers with their garden forks and cricket bats over and around the berm and I got the immense pleasure of watching the pagans screech to a halt again as doubt gripped them. With the pagans spilt in half, the half at this end were outnumbered.

The other half weren't though, and running away from me, they hadn't seen the villagers appear. I did what I felt I had to, punched my right fist into the air, and screamed like a maniac as I ran down the berm in a dead charge toward the pagans. My war cry was copied as Patience, Brad, and everyone else, sprinted toward our enemy.

The countryside of Kent is littered with ancient battlefields. It would be easy to believe that the exact piece of turf we were now converging on had seen blood shed into it before – ancient marauders meeting to fight for land or honour or whatever other nonsense they thought worthy of dying for. I just wanted my friends back.

Unarmed and outnumbered, the pagans scattered. We had divided them to conquer, the half nearest us running for the walls and scrambling over them to escape if they could. A few of the villagers got in lucky hits with a cricket bat, but most evaded our charge. They were not our target though, we were here for the prisoners, most especially the poor women who had been held captive for so long. Most of them were already released from their cages, but they were fifty yards ahead of us and even with the guards taken out, Tempest and the others had a lot of people to fight before the women would be safe.

That wasn't their only problem as the second half of the pagans were closing fast on their position. However, that half of the pagan crowd, who had been happily unaware of the threat we posed initially, heard us coming now. Some turned to face us and were bowled over, others simply got trapped and had to fight because they couldn't escape. There would be injuries on our side, I was certain of it, but as the villagers scattered the remaining half of the pagans, I could see Barbie and Jermaine. Mike would be there somewhere, and I was certain the Blue Moon boys were able to take care of themselves.

But where was the high priest?

I had to follow Tempest's line of sight to spot the chief constable as he fled. He had one hand twisted roughly into Helena Gallagher's hair and the ceremonial knife pressed to her throat. The threat of her bloodshed kept Tempest, Jermaine, and the others at bay as he backed toward the tower.

'I will not be denied my prize,' he screamed. At some point the ram's skull had been knocked off and his face mask was gone so I could see my guess had been on the money. Not that it made any difference.

Sirens in the distance told me the police were coming, but the battle here was over. Many of the pagans had escaped. Dozens had been rounded up, some were wounded and there were a few wounded villagers too, though none with anything worse than a black eye where a pagan had swung a wild punch.

Tempest shouted, 'Give it up. There's nowhere to go.' He was tracking him step for step as the chief constable backed away. Mike, Big Ben, and Jermaine were doing likewise, their hands open to show they were empty but none of them getting too close for fear of what he might do to Helena.

'Nowhere to go?' the chief constable scoffed. 'In a few minutes it will strike midnight and I won't need to go anywhere. I will become a god as Quentiox inhabits my mortal body. Then I will smite you all with my hands. You cannot stop me.'

Helena screamed for help, her cries woeful and desperate. We all wanted to help her but if we rushed him, he would cut her throat long before we could stop him.

Brad and Patience arrived. They had been tending to the other captives, the women who had been held for days and would need emotional and physical support now. Left with the villagers, they were out of danger, but Patience stormed toward the chief constable, stopped only by Big Ben snagging her arm. 'You're under arrest!' she screamed in her rage. 'How dare you? You were supposed to be the best of us, but you're just another power-hungry maniac.'

With a sneer, he replied, 'I am a god, you insignificant insect.' He acted as if we were of no consequence, but he was still backing away.

At the entrance to the tower was a wooden barrier with a danger sign attached. I could see why. On the ground around the base of the tower were rocks. Loose pieces of the thousand-year-old structure had fallen at some point in the past. At the wooden sign, he kicked out a leg, his cloak billowing as his foot connected. The sign broke and fell to the side, giving him access to the tower. He meant to climb it, dragging Helena behind him. If he got away from us, he would sacrifice her on the stroke of midnight in just a couple of minutes. What then though? He wouldn't be transformed into a mighty god and though we would then be able to subdue him, it would be too late for Helena.

'Take me,' I said before I had even considered what I was saying.

'Madam, no,' Jermaine protested.

Big Ben lunged and Helena screamed as the chief constable drew blood on her neck. Growling in his frustration, Big Ben fell back again.

I tried again. 'Take me. Let her go. It doesn't have to be her.'

He looked my way. 'Yes, you have been a pain in my side.' I could see he was considering it. I didn't have a plan; I was just trying to save a woman I'd been trying to find for days. I held my arms out to my sides and took a pace forward. He squinted his eyes in thought, but said, 'No. I think I'll stick with my original plan. This one is younger and juicier; Quentiox deserves the best I can offer.'

He took another pace, this one taking him into the shadow of the tower. Helena screamed again, but this time, with her voice echoing inside the tower, something shifted above her. Grit, sand, and fine dust fell from high above. Those of us outside saw it, but the chief constable didn't. He took another pace, disappearing further into the dark and we heard him trip.

He yelled in frustrated outrage as he tried to kick some unseen barrier out of his way. His hands were full; one holding the knife, one still wound around Helena's hair and the movement he created started a chain reaction. A rock fell from above, crashing down inside the tower. Helena screamed again and though looking back, it seems completely counter-intuitive, we all ran toward the tower, not away from it.

The first rock was followed by a second and quickly a third. Another couple fell outside, not inside, and a cry of pain told us the chief constable had been hit by something. Dust was beginning to billow out of the craggy entrance as we all converged on it, all trying to get to Helena and therefore all bowled over or knocked backward as she burst from the tower, blood leaking from a cut to her neck as she ran for her very life.

It was a sentiment the rest of us could get behind, Jermaine grabbing a handful of my clothing as he yanked me into the air. Barbie was ten yards away, but still well inside the potential kill zone of the tower if it fell.

'It's going!' she screamed as she too turned and ran.

The noise was incredible, hundreds of tons of rocks which had stood for ten centuries, came crashing down as the tower collapsed inward. A tumbling chunk of stone the size of a large dog overtook me as I told my legs to go faster than they had in many, many years. Then the dust cloud caught up to me and the world went black.

I stumbled from it moments later, helped by Jermaine who ran at my pace and refused to leave my side regardless of the danger. All around us, the faces were grimy and covered in dust, but the sound of rocks tumbling had faded to nothing more than the sound of a few pebbles settling into their new place.

I turned around to look. Where the tower had been was now a huge hole in the landscape. Illuminated by the moon, it was forever changed and somewhere inside it the chief constable for Kent was forever entombed.

Wailing sirens drew nearer and I thought of cold gin and a hot bath. With shaky hands, I took out my phone and let Jermaine help me get to Helena. She was with Patience and the other freed captives. They were hugging and crying, the women meeting each other properly for the first time now their ordeal was finally over.

I felt too weary to fight my desire to sit on the ground, using Jermaine's hand to lower myself down. 'Hello, Helena,' I said to get her attention as I touched her arm. 'My name is Patricia Fisher. Your father hired me to find you.' I gave her my phone; it was already ringing her father's number and as his voice came on the line, I heard her dissolve into a fresh bout of tears. I left her to talk with him and wondered if she even knew her husband was dead.

I hadn't got up as the flashing lights screeched to a halt and stayed where I was when the uniforms began spilling onto the grass that led up to St Leonard's Tower. I could hear Chief Inspector Quinn calling for me or Tempest alternately. Then PC Brad Hardacre found him, escorting him to where our small group were resting on the side of the berm. It gave us a good view of everything, and we had unanimously decided we were too tired to move. We had managed to find some scraps of clothing to borrow, villagers giving up coats to cover up those of us still in our underwear. At least I had a coat, Barbie was in a tiny bra and thong, the guys in briefs.

Many of the villagers had already gone home, but a lot had hung around, too fired up from the excitement of the fight to return home just when the police were arriving.

Chief Inspector Quinn covered the last few yards and then saw what we were wearing. He looked at each of us and just shook his head. 'I feel I should be arresting you all for indecent exposure. Mrs Fisher, I should definitely arrest you and Mr Clarke for smashing your way into a business in Canterbury. You are no doubt going to tell me that it was all to achieve the rescue tonight.'

I didn't answer straight away. Paramedics had arrived to treat the women and take them away and they each wanted to take a moment to thank us once again for saving them. Chief Inspector Quinn remained quiet until they were gone. They would be well looked after and reunited with their families – my part in their story was at an end. The story I needed to tell now, was that of the chief constable and how he came to be the head of a murderous cult.

He hadn't attended Hartford Boys' Academy. Had he done so I believe it would have sent my senses twitching long before it did. He went to a local comprehensive school close to Hartford Boys' Academy, but the connection was his father who had been a religious studies teacher there and taught all the boys including David Sebastian. One of the religions his father taught was paganism and it had resonated with his own son who went on to study it himself at university. Tempest's colleague Jane had provided me with a simple bullet point breakdown at my request. I didn't know much, but I knew all I needed to know to be certain it was him inside the ram's skull. His dissertation had been on a lesser known pagan god called Quentiox.

The men Albert Brady chose to elevate in his cult all ran businesses which had boomed in the last few years. An investigation into their affairs would reveal that for each of them, their main rival or rivals had suffered police raids where illegal activity had been found. Some had large quantities of drugs found on the premises, others were accused of money laundering and though each protested their innocence, they were unable to continue trading which left men like Anthony Perkins to thrive in a competition-free market. Chief Constable of Kent Police, Albert Brady was behind the case and the cover ups, though there had to be others within the service who were guilty of carrying out his orders. Chief Inspector Quinn believed the investigation might go on for years.

Frank went home breathing a huge sigh of relief and remained convinced we had prevented the end of the world. Tempest's girlfriend, who had been away investigating another case, appeared at the tower site to be with him, and Mike was given his job back on the spot – the chief constable's decision to fire him no longer worth anything so far as CI Quinn was concerned.

The other, and very vital, piece of information I got from Jane Butterworth was to do with what connected the chief constable to Ivor Biggun. The answer, it transpired, was simple. Albert Brady's daughter was one of Ivor Biggun's actresses and he took exception to it. It had been his influence as head of Kent Police as David Sebastian ran for office that caused David to focus a campaign against the internet mogul. However, when the lord mayor failed to bring him down, Albert Brady went a stage further, using his contacts and influences to make the bombs. Quinn said it might be hard to tie it to the chief constable, but I believed the cult members would start talking soon enough. In fact, I thought it likely the police would have a complete list of every member in no time at all and be making a record number of arrests that would make Quinn look very good indeed.

When I finished laying it all out for the chief inspector, he drew in a deep breath through his nose and exhaled it again slowly. 'I feel I must congratulate you, Mrs Fisher. Were it not for your tenacity, I fear the chief constable would not have been caught.'

'Don't forget the foiled bombing,' Big Ben reminded him.

'And the rescued hostages,' added Barbie.

Tempest wasn't to be left out either. 'And the end of a murder spree.'

Patience opened her mouth to add something, but Quinn's hard stare stopped her; she still had to work with him tomorrow.

'Yes. I think we can all agree, Mrs Fisher ...'

'And Blue Moon Investigations,' Jermaine added quickly.

Chief Inspector Quinn sighed. 'Yes, and Blue Moon, saved the day on this occasion. Mrs Fisher, in fact, all of you, will need to give a preliminary statement to one of my officers before you leave this site. Later today, you will need to come to Maidstone police station to record a formal statement. I ask that you do not make us chase you.'

With a yawn, Tempest said, 'Yes, yes, Chief Inspector. We know the drill.' That seemed to about wrap things up. We were free to go and there was nothing to keep us sitting around in the cool night air at the ruins of St Leonard's Tower.

So we didn't. Tempest and I hugged, which started a group hug as we all rejoiced that we were still alive. Then, Jermaine, Barbie and I walked home, declining the offer of a lift for the peaceful five-minute stroll. It was gone two when we got in, yet Jermaine still tried to tend to my needs first. I sent him to bed and Barbie too, then poured a large measure of gin with some tonic and went for a bath that I desperately needed. I could only just remember patting Anna and falling into bed.

Barbie came to check on me at seven o'clock the next morning. I was asleep until she knocked on my door but shook off my slumber as she poked her head around the door. 'Hey, Patty,' she beamed. 'I wasn't sure if you were awake.'

'I am now,' I moaned, then under my breath added, 'You hateful cow.'

'Did you say something?' she asked, sweeping into my room as she stretched her arms above her head and behind her back.

I mumbled, 'No, I was just yawning.' I knew why she was here. We exercised five mornings a week. It was our routine and I had asked - can you believe that? - asked that she make me get up and do it and not suffer my excuses, so here she was, in my bedroom, obeying my wishes.

I was so stupid. Chirpily she said, 'I thought we could both do with a lie in today, so you got a whole extra hour in bed.'

172

I narrowed my eyes at her. 'I didn't go to bed until after three this morning. That's less than four hours ago. Doesn't that count?'

She chuckled. 'Of course it counts, silly. That's why I didn't wake you at six thirty. See you downstairs in five.'

I groaned again and rolled over to bury my face in the pillows. Forty-five minutes later, we arrived back at the house from our morning run; me looking like I had fallen through a hedge and into a puddle as usual, Barbie looking like she had just left a photoshoot for a sportswear company. I showered, dressed, and ate a sensible yet sustaining breakfast. Then I walked around my garden with Anna and her pups, taking the little ones outside now that they were inoculated against the full range of canine diseases. Mostly I was trying to delay a task I really didn't want to do. Last night I accused the lord mayor of Kent of being a crazy pagan god worshipping murderer. Worse yet, I lured him to a room with the promise of sex where I had my faithful butler knock him out and then we tied him up and abandoned him. Now I needed to call him and apologise. I would have done it last night, but it was gone midnight by the time I got the chance and the police had just arrived. I ran the whole case through my head again from start to finish as I made a second circuit of my garden but knew I couldn't put the unwelcome task off any longer. Settling onto a handy stone bench, I called the number I had for David Sebastian and waited for it to connect.

'Good morning, Patricia.' His words were short and clipped; he was being polite, but he didn't feel that he needed to be.

'Good morning, David,' I replied, wondering if I ought to sound more humble and address him as lord mayor. 'I am calling to apologise for last night. I misread a number of clues and believed that you were the high priest of the cult you no doubt saw on the news this morning.'

173

'I'm going to stop you right there,' he interrupted rudely though I had no position to complain about his behaviour or attitude; I was the one in the wrong. 'I know what you were trying to do and who you were up against. I received a full report this morning. That you were successful amazes me, but it doesn't excuse knocking me out and tying me to a desk in a house which then exploded.'

I mumbled, 'No, David,'

'So, this Friday night, I shall be taking you on a date.'

I jerked like I had been jabbed with a cattle prod. 'I'm sorry?' I said, sure I must have misheard him.

'A date, Patricia. One date. Dinner, a glass of wine, some light, non-assault and battery related conversation. I believe you owe me that much.' He was chuckling now, finding amusement in my discomfort and surprise. 'If, after that, you really don't want to see me again, then I will get the message.'

Feeling a little stunned, I stuttered, 'I, ah, I don't know what to say.'

'I think agreeing to my proposition would be a good start. Or, you know, I could consider it my moral duty to report the attack on me last night. I'm sure the police would be very interested to hear about a public dignitary being molested in public.'

My cheeks had to be glowing bright red with the heat I could feel coming off them. I genuinely didn't know how to feel about going on a date with him, but he was handsome and well-groomed and held a position of public responsibility. Plus, I had no romantic ties other than to a man who I might never see again. I said, 'Yes, David. I would love to.'

'Super. I shall send a car for you at eight. I believe there are some Michelin starred restaurants near you. Perhaps you could wear the outfit from last night again, I rather liked it.'

My eyes widened in shock. 'Um,'

'Only joking,' he laughed. 'About wearing it, I mean. I really did like it. Eight o'clock Friday. Expect more flowers.' He disconnected and I had to lower my head because I felt woozy.

To myself, I asked, 'What the heck just happened?' I couldn't allow myself the time I wanted to dwell on it though, I already had another case to look into and clients waiting for results.

The End

Except it isn't. There's a whole load more over the page.

Book 3 in Patricia Fisher's Mystery Adventures

You might think murder would be rare in a quiet English village ...

When the local goddess of cake is found impaled with her own palette knife, the victim's husband is found holding the murder weapon. It's an open and shut case ...

... until he calls Patricia Fisher that is.

With a surprising new assistant in tow, your favourite middle-aged sleuth has all the help she will need, but this case is a tough one for everyone she suspects instantly becomes the next victim.

With the village fete a week away, cooks are revving up to win the coveted best cake prize, especially now that the favourite is in the morgue. Can the killer really be one of the lovely old ladies?

With president of the church council, old rival Angelica Howard-Box, stirring up trouble, Patricia has more than enough on her plate, and she'll have to solve this fast because her own cook, Mrs Pam Ellis might be next!

Click the link embedded in the cover picture above to continue your adventure right now!

Baking. It can get a guy killed.

When a retired detective superintendent chooses to take a culinary tour of the British Isles, he hopes to find tasty treats and delicious bakes …

… what he finds is a clue to a crime in the ingredients for his pork pie.

His dog, Rex Harrison, an ex-police dog fired for having a bad attitude, cannot understand why the humans are struggling to solve the mystery. He can already smell the answer – it's right before their noses.

He'll pitch in to help his human and the shop owner's teenage daughter as the trio set out to save the shop from closure. Is the rival pork pie shop across the street to blame? Or is there something far more sinister going on?

One thing is for sure, what started out as a bit of fun, is getting deadlier by the hour, and they'd better work out what the dog knows soon or it could be curtains for them all.

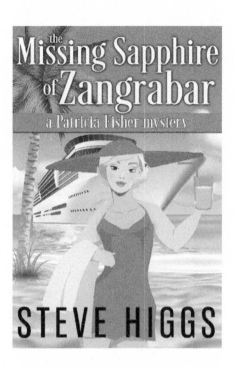

Read the book that started it all.

A thirty-year-old priceless jewel theft and a man who really has been stabbed in the back. Can a 52-year-old, slightly plump housewife unravel the mystery in time to save herself from jail?

When housewife, Patricia, catches her husband in bed with her best friend, her reaction isn't to rant and yell. Instead, she calmly empties the bank accounts and boards the first cruise ship in nearby Southampton.

There she meets the unfairly handsome captain and her appointed butler for the trip – that's what you get when the only room available is a royal suite! But with most of the money gone and sleeping off a gin-fuelled pity party for one, she wakes to find herself accused of murder; she was seen leaving the bar with the victim and her purse is in his cabin.

Certain that all she did last night was fall into bed, a race against time begins as she tries to work out what happened and clear her name. But the deputy captain, the man responsible for safety and security onboard, has confined her to her cabin and has no interest in her version of events. Worse yet, as she begins to dig into the dead man's past, she uncovers a secret - there's a giant stolen sapphire somewhere and people are prepared to kill to get their hands on it.

With only a Jamaican butler faking an English accent and a pretty gym instructor to help, she must piece together the clues and do it fast. Or when she gets off the ship in St Kitts, she'll be in cuffs!

Even More Books by Steve Higgs

Blue Moon Investigations

Paranormal Nonsense

The Phantom of Barker Mill

Amanda Harper Paranormal Detective

The Klowns of Kent

Dead Pirates of Cawsand

In the Doodoo With Voodoo

The Witches of East Malling

Crop Circles, Cows and Crazy Aliens

Whispers in the Rigging

Bloodlust Blonde – a short story

Paws of the Yeti

Under a Blue Moon – A Paranormal Detective Origin Story

Night Work

Lord Hale's Monster

Herne Bay Howlers

Undead Incorporated

Albert Smith's Culinary Chronicles

Pork Pie Pandemonium

Bakewell Tart Bludgeoning

Stilton Slaughter

Patricia Fisher Cruise Mysteries

The Missing Sapphire of Zangrabar

The Kidnapped Bride

The Director's Cut

The Couple in Cabin 2124

Doctor Death

Murder on the Dancefloor

Mission for the Maharaja

A Sleuth and her Dachshund in Athens

The Maltese Parrot

No Place Like Home

Patricia Fisher Mystery Adventures

What Sam Knew

Solstice Goat

Recipe for Murder

A Banshee and a Bookshop

Diamonds, Dinner Jackets, and Death

Frozen Vengeance

The Realm of False Gods

Untethered magic

Unleashed Magic

Early Shift

Damaged but Powerful

Demon Bound

Familiar Territory

Author Note:

Thank you for reading my book, I hope you enjoyed it. Writing it was certainly fun, the story flowing easily from my head to the page in little more than a week as I started each day long before the rest of my family, or even the sun, thought about getting up. If you are new to Patricia, then welcome. For everyone else, welcome back.

I never thought of myself as a cozy mystery writer. Whenever I fantasised about a career as a novelist, I always pictured myself writing fantasy or action adventure, but a chance event lead to the creation of Patricia Fisher and here we are twelve books and a novella later with another twenty one books currently planned for her and a culinary cozy series taking shape.

It is early March 2020 as I craft this final note, my son and wife are in the living room watching Mickey Mouse and enjoying a more gentle start to their day. It is cool in the house which has me blowing on my fingers to keep them warm and everyone else under a blanket with our three dachshunds. Spring is almost upon us which means my garden is coming back to life, but the cold weather hasn't quite left us yet and my animal-mad four-year-old wants to be outside most of the time.

Tomorrow, he and I will be clad in wellington boots and layered up to attend a local farm club which is the cutest two hours of my week. Last week the lambs were being born so he got to pet them and feed them and then return home to care for Barbara, our oldest and most wobbly chicken. We rescued some battery hens a while back, they don't lay eggs anymore, but they cluck around and give him endless hours of pleasure as he digs up earth worms to feed them. Barbara probably wasn't getting her share of the food, so during the recent cold period, she slept in the house in a cage with food, water, and warmth. My son thought that was great, and so did the dachshunds who are rather partial to a bit of roast chicken. Thankfully, Hunter, my son, is wise enough to keep the two separated.

I have an urban fantasy book to write next, so this Patricia adventure is heading off to the proofreading team as I open a notebook and start to plot.

Take care

Steve Higgs

Get sneak peaks, exclusive giveaways, behind the scenes content, and more. Plus, you'll be notified of Fan Pricing events when they occur and get exclusive offers from other authors because all UF writers are automatically friends.

Not only that, but you'll receive an exclusive FREE story staring Otto and Zachary and two free stories from the author's Blue Moon Investigations series.

Yes, please! Sign me up for lots of FREE stuff and bargains!

Want to follow me and keep up with what I am doing?

Facebook

Made in the USA
Coppell, TX
13 June 2022

78797501R00111